Praise for Grant Jerkins

"Brilliant. Brutal. Hitchcockian. Endlessly fascinating."
—*Savannah Morning News*

"Dark. Chilling. Startling. No one is as they appear to be, and the twists and turns never let up."
—*Library Journal* (Starred Review)

"You have to admire the purity of Jerkins's writing: He's determined to peer into the darkness and tell us exactly what he sees."
—*The Washington Post*

"Dares us to solve a mystery in which none of the normal character cues can be taken at face value."
—*The New York Times Book Review*

"Grisly suspense. Unimaginable horror."
—*Kirkus Reviews*

"Jerkins juggles his plot twists like a top circus acrobat."
—***Publishers Weekly*** (*A Very Simple Crime*)

"Maliciously cunning. Ratchets up a high level of dread."
—***Publisher's Weekly*** (*At the End of the Road*)

"Darkly comic, consistently surprising, and agreeably macabre."
—***Publisher's Weekly*** (*The Ninth Step*)

"Gritty, sordid, disturbing, and addictive."
—***Richmond Times-Dispatch***

"Reminiscent of classic thrillers—from Psycho to Deliverance to Whatever Happened to Baby Jane to Lord of the Flies."
—***Atlanta Journal Constitution***

"Unravels with an unstoppable momentum."
—***Barnes & Noble Ransom Notes***

"Absolutely pitch-perfect."
—***The Florida Times-Union***

"Irresistibly nerve-racking."
—***Kirkus Reviews***

"[His novels] keep you in their grip and leave you thinking about the story and characters long afterwards."

—*Stay Curious*

"Gripping. Chilling. Unexpected. The writing is top-notch. His stories have been compared to Hitchcock movies because they take ordinary people into the dark, criminal edges."

— *Minneapolis Star Tribune*

"So stylishly twisted that I read it in one sitting."

—*Milwaukee Journal Sentinel* (Top 10 List)

"An absolutely fearless writer."

—*Elizabeth A. White*

"Gets to the heart of some my favorite themes: guilt, obsession, and redemption are all organically breached and beautifully handled in this agonizing, character-driven thriller."

—*Spinetingler Magazine*

"A thriller you can't put down. The unsettling feeling of something always being a little off starts on page one."

—*The Windy Page*

ALSO BY GRANT JERKINS

A Very Simple Crime

At the End of the Road

The Ninth Step

Done in One

Abnormal Man

A Scholar of Pain

VIVIEN, AFTER

GRANT JERKINS

EDEN ROAD BOOKS

If you purchased this book without a cover, you should be aware that this book is stolen property. It was reported as "unsold and destroyed" to the publisher, and neither the author nor the publisher has received any payment for this "stripped book."

VIVIEN, AFTER

Eden Road Books / published by arrangement with the author

All rights reserved
Copyright © 2026 by Grant Jerkins

This book may not be reproduced in whole or in part in any form without permission.

For information address: Eden Road Books,
200 Madison Avenue, New York, New York 10016

Cover art Copyright© 2026 Kyle Edwards

This is a work of fiction. The events, characters, names, locations, and incidents described are either the product of the author's imagination or are used fictitiously. Any resemblance to actual persons, living or dead, or to actual events, locales, or organizations is entirely coincidental.

ISBN: 979-8-9946355-0-6 (Paperback)
ISBN: 979-8-9946355-3-7 (Red Letter Edition, Paperback)
ISBN: 979-8-9946355-1-3 (Red Letter Edition, Hardcover)
ISBN: 979-8-9946355-2-0 (eBook)

Eden Road Books®
Eden Road Books are published by the New Earth Publishing Group,
200 Madison Avenue, New York, New York 10016

New Earth, Eden Road Books, and the ERB design
are trademarks belonging to New Earth Publishing Corporation.

Printed in the United States of America
10 9 8 7 6 5 4 3 2 1

For my brother, Jeff Jerkins
And my father, A.N. Jerkins
Two sides of the same coin

Contents

{} 1

{α} 3

The Dark Player (*Won't You Meet ME*) 9

Imagine There's No People 13

Tails, You Lose 23

The Best Prize 25

The Divine Game 29

Murder and Other So-Called Misdeeds 33

Disidentification 37

The End of ME 41

Observe the Observer (*When I's Dead and Gone*) 43

A Very Simple Philosophy 49

The Web and the Rock 57

Abomination 63

A Hole in the Earth and a Vessel in the Sky 67

The Sacred Stillness of the Present Moment 73

The Knack and How to Get It 79

So Sweet the Means of Death 85

Ceaseless Chatter 89

These Things Are Preprogrammed into Us 111

Journey to Enlightenment 115

In the Midst of Heaven (*Meet ME in the Middle of the Air*) . 121

A Vector of Blame 125

Escape from Emptiness 127

Nothing At All 131

Dear Vivien, Won't You Come Out to Play? 135

Bette Davis Eyes 139

This Woman Is Very Much Dead 145

She Waits the Consummation 149

Reflections in a Golden Eye 155

The Suffering Goes on Forever 173

A Sober Person	181
Synchronicity	187
No Mask to Wear	199
A Rather Unpleasant Jewel	203
The Eckhart Tolle Murder Club	209
The Blood of Jesus	211
A Moon for the Misbegotten	217
Flashpoint	221
It Makes You Feel Good	225
Three Two One	227
No Guru	231
Sanctuary	235
As I Lay Dying	237
How to Be Born Again:	247
{1} *Don't Want Nobody to Moan*	249
{2} *True Religion in My Heart*	253
{3} *Goin' on Down to the River*	267
Ω	285
Afterword	289

{}

S*WIRL.*
The stars spun and the Dark Player moved. The dream of form began.

It was a cunning move from a cunning opponent. A long con—or a short grift—depending on one's perspective.

{α}

THE BEING EXISTED IN PHYSICAL FORM.

    If there was a creator who had created the being, the being did not know. Nor did it wonder. Perhaps the being created itself. But the being was unaware it existed. It did not think. It was surrounded by other, similar beings. The first birthed the second. The second birthed the first. A deluge of single-cell life.

    It responded to light. It was drawn to light.

    It did not know there was water or sky or land.

    It did not know there was an abyss.

    Darkness came. The physical form died.

• • •

The being existed in physical form on dry land. The being did not know the land was dry. It did not know there was night and day, wet and dry, land and sky.

It was drawn to the light.

The rain was wet, and the being put down roots to anchor itself so it could grow tall and drink the rain. The light covered it. It responded to the rain and responded to the light.

As its roots grew into the soil, its branches reached toward the sky.

The rain did not come for a very long time, and the land became arid.

The being did not mind this.

Without water, the physical form died.

The being did not mind this, either.

• • •

The being sunned itself on a rock. It was drawn to the light.

Warmed, the being scurried away to a nearby creek. The being knew water was there. The being had a rudimentary memory. It knew where the creek was, but it did not know it knew this.

In the sacred stillness of the present moment, the being waited patiently. It waited for food. It did not know it was waiting. It had no concept of future. It had no concept of past. There was only the timeless now. Its tongue slithered from its mouth, perhaps in anticipation, perhaps not. It waited. Eyes half-lidded, it waited, and its reptilian brain thought no-thoughts.

The being could wait for months. It could die for lack of food, but it would not care.

Today, however, there was food. A fly buzzed nearby, and the lizard's tongue darted out and caught the fly.

The being that existed in the physical form of the fly died. Its dream of form ended.

The reptile resumed its patient wait for more food.

It could wait forever. Because it did not know it was waiting.

A cross-shaped shadow passed over the reptile. The threat slipped silently overhead, not even a whisper, and then the shadow returned. The lizard's brain lit up with a signal of danger. The reptilian brain had already sent an impulse for the legs to flee. As fast as possible—flee.

But it was too late. The eagle's talons were long and sharp and punctured the lizard's scaled flesh, killing it even as its legs jerked—midair—in motions of escape.

For the lizard, the dream of form ended.

The eagle soared.

· · ·

The being existed in the physical form of a woman. The woman was part of a group. The group wandered in deserts and on mountains, hiding in caves, dens, and holes. Today, they lived in a dark underground cavern. They scavenged outside. Because they were scavengers, and because they were drawn to the light.

The woman had no name. None of them had names. They had something like titles. When one died, another replaced the dead one and was called by that same title.

The woman was a seer. Her title, uttered, sounded like Maddocks. *She was not the leader of the tribe. The leader was a man. The men killed one another to briefly be the leader.*

Maddocks was aligned with the stars. Things happened for her—luck—and she knew certain information even though she had no way of knowing it. She was not the leader, but in many ways, she had more power than any man.

On the ground, she scattered smooth pebbles or fragile bones or fresh bloody entrails and foretold the future by the patterns she saw there.

The bones she scattered were small. They could have been rodent bones, or, perhaps, the thin, hollow bones of a bird. But they were not.

She communicated in grunts, awkward verbal articulations, and graceful hand gestures. It was a language the world never recorded. A language that would die when this tribe died, its last few members

VIVIEN, AFTER

assimilated and bred by stronger, more intelligent tribes that had their own coarse languages that would also die without record.

Words. Maddocks *knew that all words were symbols. Words stood for things, but they were not those things.*

She was barren. The word for barren was also maddocks.

A girl was stolen from another tribe and bred by the men of Maddocks's tribe, one after another, until the girl's belly swelled. Maddocks foretold an abomination. Using word-symbols, she told her tribe a curse was coming. Maddocks told them the fruit was blighted. She pointed to the scattered stones, the fragile bones that were not rodent bones, and the ink-red entrails, reading their patterns of impending doom. Her head hummed with it.

And she gestured to the stars, where the gods lived, the ill omen displayed there as well. The pattern was obvious. She pointed to a supernova, shining its beacon of warning from 400 light years away, and demanded the gestation be stopped. She knew how. But the men refused.

Maddocks was proved right. The birth should have taken a matter of minutes, but the girl labored all night and much of the next day. Using primitive tools of wood and bone, Maddocks urged the fetus out. She wielded the coarse instruments to widen the birth canal and massage the uterine walls. The tools ruined the girl. She would never again bear a child. Later, the tribe called her Maddocks, *too.*

What finally issued forth from the girl's womb was indeed a blight on the tribe—malformed and hideous.

Maddocks picked up a rock (a rough orb of striped granite) and crushed the infant's fragile head. An infant that had not yet made a crying noise, because it was incapable of crying.

She folded its dying arms, gnawed through the cord, and thrust the untethered, unwanted clump of glistening tissue out to the girl.

Woman, here is your son.

An accusation. A condemnation. Because the girl wasn't a woman, and what she had birthed wasn't human. Not really.

Maddocks slung the funiculus high into the calcium sky—toward a soaring bird—and discarded the carcass into a hole in the earth. An abyss. She would scavenge the bones later.

For the being birthed by the captive girl, the dream of form ended.

The Dark Player
(*Won't You Meet ME*)

THE WOMAN WHO EXISTED IN THE PHYSICAL FORM CALLED Vivien Williams sat down at her bedroom desk and prepared to write. Her head was humming, and she couldn't get it to stop. She hoped the act of writing might ease the vibration.

Words, she knew, were symbols. The humming was energy.

She chose this spot to write because beyond the window, a malodorous water branch cut through the property, past a nearby weeping cherry tree, where there was a songbird who sings.

She hadn't seen that songbird in quite a while. Years. Nor had she heard it. Or felt joy from its sweet, simple trill. She wasn't sure if the songbird was really gone, or if her heart had grown callous, her hearing dull. If she had shut her eyes and couldn't see.

Vivien heard rain. She got up, opened the window, looked out and thought, *the devil is beating his wife*.

From a clear blue sky, raindrops—bright blazing water vessels—descended like iron nails through the dazzling sunlight that streamed over the top of the cherry tree. A sunshower. Each water-nail pierced the reflective, membranous surface of the stagnate creek and drenched the bedroom with hypnotic swirls of shimmering light.

Vivien was drawn to light.

She was part of a group called a family. Many families lived in suburban houses in the neighborhoods of the metro-Atlanta area of Georgia. Her sister lived in one house and Vivien lived in another. They each had subfamilies. In addition to this, Vivien's husband led a group of men and women within the larger community. Her husband was a sort of guru.

Vivien now reflected that she intended to cause grievous harm to her family, her subfamily, and to the community as a whole. Her actions might, one could posit, harm humanity itself. There was also a case to be made that what she contemplated could, paradoxically, help the cause of humanity. But you had to hold the situation to the light, squint, and look at it just right in order to think of Vivien's plan as a good one.

Logically, what she intended was a bad idea.

She, herself, had given up logic. Thinking. Judging. Moralizing. The idea of good or bad, right or wrong, life or death. Those were just words.

So much death. There would be blood on her hands. But she didn't know if the blood would be an indictment or an anointment.

So much pain and death. The suffering went on forever.

Vivien closed the window. The songbird was nowhere to be found. Perhaps it didn't like the rain. She wished it would come back. Someday, maybe.

She missed that songbird.

Last spring, she took a stepladder and climbed to the top of the dwarf tree. Sure enough, there was a nest. Brittle pine straw. Three eggs. The eggs were reticulated, crazed, pierced in spots. Battered, but still whole. No predator had gotten to the eggs. They looked purposefully damaged. Like tiny, crushed skulls. Vivien knew a bird might shatter its own eggs, perceiving them as defective or otherwise undesirable. Unwanted. So they destroyed them. But what kind of animal did such a thing?

Sitting back down to her desk, she cleared her mind. No more thoughts of songbirds, reticulated eggs, or wife-beating devils.

She thought no-thoughts. Her head hummed like a tuning fork, and her pupils constricted oddly.

She wrote, *what is the purpose of life?*

Imagine There's No People

WHAT IS THE PURPOSE OF LIFE?

What is the meaning of life? What is the point? Why are we here? Why am *I* here?

They are all the same question.

A better question might be: Why do we ask the question at all?

I can tell you who doesn't ask this question: happy people.

People rocketing down a water slide. People on a roller coaster. This is why we're thrill-seekers. Because a thrill is the ultimate release from our everyday worries. A thrill makes us happy. A good laugh does the same thing. Happy people never ask about the purpose of life. They are too busy enjoying life to question its purpose.

Most of us don't ask this question during the first decade of our life. Nor do we typically require an explanation of existence during our second decade. For many, youth tends to be a time of happiness. Or, perhaps more likely, we are content with the explanation our caregivers gave us before we ever had the chance to ask—namely, that the purpose of life is to serve God (in one form or another).

From the age of one to twenty, we're content with *being*. We don't require a purpose (a grand scheme) to enjoy the act of living. Nor do we require a purpose to loathe suffering. Or to celebrate pleasure. We simply suffer without thought as to why, just as we experience pleasure without thought as to why. It's all living, it's all being, and we require no explanation. The five-year-old who stubs their toe doesn't wonder *what's the point of living if I must experience this pain?* They wail and seek comfort—a Band-Aid applied, preferably with a mother's kiss—and keep on living. Teens kissing in a car don't stop to wonder what's the point to any of this. They just know it makes you feel good and that is enough.

Then, sometime after adolescence, many of us begin to desire an explanation. There are exceptions. Childhood depressives, teenage existential crises. Juvenile carcinomas, high-school pregnancies. These can put a damper on youthful glee, but there is therapy for mental illness, cancers are largely treatable, and expectant sophomores can get the problem addressed by having their older sister take them to a cash-on-demand family planning clinic. These events might be ruminated upon later in life, but it underlines my argument that, as we enter adulthood, that's when we start to question it. This thing I've been doing my entire life, this suffering, this happiness, this work and reward, this family and friends, this solitude and contemplation—this act of being—why am I doing it? Why are any of us doing it?

When we ask ourselves *what is the purpose of life?* what we really mean is *what is the purpose of* human *life?* When we ask *why am I here?* by association and inclusion we also ask, *why are* we *here?* All of us. Humans. What purpose do we serve, being human beings, being.

Suppose for a minute that humanity didn't exist. Just imagine. As John Lennon pointed out, it's easy if you try. So just imagine. Imagine planet earth exactly as it is now, but with no human beings going around improving things.

There are still cats and dogs, eagles and vultures, fish and whales, trees and algae, rain and wind and clouds. But no man. So, what now? Does life still require a purpose? Imagine you were a god (or even *The* God) and stumbled upon (or created) this lovely blue planet, throbbing with glorious, unimaginably diverse life. Would you wonder, *what's the point?* What's the purpose of all this beauty? Maybe, you as a god would decide to create a new creature, a new life form, and while you're at it create this new life form in your own image. Call this new life form Man. Male and female. So they can reproduce through the ephemeral bliss of physical union. Give Man a soul while you're at it. And set Man down onto this life-filled world. And now, *now*, you've given the world purpose.

Imagine. It's easy if you try.

Of course, that's biblical. Theological. If you believed that, you wouldn't be here having this discourse with me. You wouldn't be poking and prodding and massaging this question. Because you already know the purpose of life is to serve God (in one form or another.) Be fruitful and multiply. Like adolescents in a parked car.

I'm not being facetious or condescending. Not at all. I'm married to a Baptist preacher. Most of my family call themselves Christian—all of them, as far as I know. Some of them just pose as Christians. And several of them have the faith to go along with the title. They have a firm, unyielding belief in the omnipotent, omniscient God and His Son, Jesus Christ, through who's sacrifice believers are Saved and will reap the reward of eternal life.

The rest will burn in a lake of fire. Forever.

VIVIEN, AFTER

I heard an interesting description of hell. Picture a mountain—bigger than Everest. A mountain of granite. Now imagine that once every 10,000 years a sparrow alights on the mountain to sharpen its beak for a few moments and then flutters away. Imagine how much time it would take for that sparrow to wear that mountain down, to grind it to dust by sharpening its beak once every decamillennium. That—that amount of time—will be the end of the first second, of the first minute, of the first hour, of your first day in hell.

That's quite a long time.

And good inducement to accept Jesus Christ as your personal Lord and Savior.

We're not here to talk about religion. Let's get back to our beautiful planet, abundant with non-human life. Does that non-human life have a purpose? Does it *require* a purpose? For itself, I do not believe it requires a purpose. An eagle, soaring majestically in a blue sky, does not require a purpose. It simply soars.

You could say that the purpose of non-human life is to serve humans (as our purpose is to serve God), and you might have a point. A dog, for example, may serve the purpose of providing companionship to man. As a chicken provides food. (And we're not restricting this thought puzzle to animal life. Plants serve a purpose as well. In fact, many cultures believe stones, crystals, trees, etc., house spirits.)

This idea that all lesser forms of life are here to serve man seems biblical in origin, but if we are going on the assumption that man is somehow *special*, and thus all other life really is less-than, then it's reasonable (not biblical) to say the purpose of all other life is to serve man.

Which splits our original question into two questions: What is the purpose of (all) life? And what is the purpose of (human) life? And perhaps a third, what is the purpose of (my) life?

Let's start with that last question. It's almost a throwaway. Trivial. *What is the purpose of (my) life?* The answer is: whatever gives you a sense of purpose—that is the purpose of your life. (Again, I think you would be better off asking yourself why you *need* a purpose—examine *that*—but if you feel you require a purpose to give your life meaning, then by all means, have one.) But realize that you are putting yourself above all other life forms. You assert that you are special. A tree does not require a purpose, but you do. What makes your life more significant than a tree's life? If you are objecting to this, saying, *no, no I don't believe my life is more meaningful than the life of a tree or a goat or a chimpanzee*; then I must point out that your question isn't What is the purpose of (my) life? Your question is What is the purpose of (all) life?

And if you are not objecting, if you are nodding in agreement that yes, you are indeed somehow special, your life is light-years more important than the life of a tree or a goat or a chimpanzee—

then you can stop reading. You know the purpose of your life. This is wonderful news. Mission accomplished. This is an epiphany. If you believe your life is more important than a tree's life (more meaningful and therefore requiring a purpose to merit that meaning), then you believe the purpose of the tree's life is either non-existent or somehow less-than your purpose. (Assuming there is an almanac somewhere ranking the importance of life-meanings, your purpose and the tree's purpose would be duly catalogued, and your purpose would rank (if not at the top) well above a tree's purpose.)

Or, if you simply believe your life has a purpose and a tree's does not, then the purpose of a tree must be to serve you (by providing you cooling shade, or wood to build shelter, or sweet fruit to fill your belly). If that's the case, then your purpose is to serve whatever is above you in the spiritual food chain. Whatever it is that ranks above you in the almanac. And if it turns out that mankind really is the king of the universe, with no life forms ranking above us, then your purpose is to serve yourself (in one form or another). That form could be altruistic, or self-aggrandizing. It's up to you. Follow your bliss.

And if you're prone to self-reflection, as you saunter away content in your life's purpose, you might ask yourself which lifeform makes the judgement of which lifeforms are special? Who wrote that almanac? It just so happens that human beings, the only beings capable of making complex judgements, are the ones making the judgement that of all the known lifeforms in existence, human beings are the most highly evolved—the most special. Now, we are not without modesty, we humans, we will acknowledge that it's a biased decision, so we turn that decision over to a higher power. We turn that decision over to God, and it just so happens that God's decision, God's judgement, is that man is indeed special. Special enough to have an eternal soul.

If it turns out that God did not create man, but rather that man created God, and this God we created just happens to believe that mankind is His greatest creation, then we're right back where we started from. We're self-appointing ourselves as special. Just as birds or squirrels would.

Orwell saw this when he wrote all animals are created equal, but some are more equal than others.

● ● ●

Let's continue working backward through our three questions.

Two: What is the purpose of (human) life?

I must concede, the question is unanswerable (at least by me, at the present moment.) The question assumes that humans have a unique purpose and human life is somehow more important than the life of any other animal. And certainly, it is. At least to humans. Just as, to cows, bovine life is more important than, say, lupine life. If you are mentally objecting to this train of thought, saying that just because you believe humanity has a different purpose—not necessarily a *better* purpose—then you, reader, are implying that every life form has its own unique purpose.

Let's ask the amoeba.

Tails, You Lose

WHAT IS DEATH? LIFE AND DEATH ARE TWO SIDES OF THE SAME coin. Inseparable. One and the same. Quite literally, you can't have one without the other. So, why do we fear death? We cannot experience life without death, so why would we fear it? Why would we fear the very thing that makes life possible? To fear death is to fear life. Do you see what I'm getting at? Fearing death taints our lives because it is insanity to fear the thing that makes life possible. How can you relish life if you're constantly worried about death?

Well, why shouldn't we? We're all going to die—and soon. It's all going to end in death. Life, by its very definition, is impermanent. It's only one side of the coin that we flip every day of our lives. And eventually, that coin is going to come up tails. So why bother flipping at all? What's the point? The game is rigged. It's rigged and you're guaranteed to lose. So, I repeat, what's the point?

There is no point. Not if you believe death is the end. No point at all. After years of searching for an answer, that's the conclusion I came up with.

Unless you believe enlightenment is possible. That we transcend death. It is said that enlightenment is the end of suffering. We are born and reborn seeking enlightenment—an end to this cycle of suffering. Each new life offers a new path to enlightenment.

If that's true, then murder is a sacred act.

The Best Prize

THERE IS NO PURPOSE. NOT FOR ME, THE INDIVIDUAL.

The conclusion I've drawn (and I can only speak for myself) is that life (itself) has a purpose. Indeed, it does. How could it not? Human life, however, does not have a unique or celestial or divinely bestowed purpose. Ipso facto, my individual life serves no purpose beyond the purpose of life itself. I serve on the same plane as the amoeba. As do you.

And yet, I crave purpose.

Me—I end at the skin. I am inside my skin. Eckhart Tolle or Alan Watts or one of those mystics might say that the biological me is indeed inside the skin. But the entirety of me does not end at the epidermis. Here's the thing, you can't have an inside without an outside. Just as you can't have life without death. So, Mr. Tolle might ask, what is outside your skin? The answer? *Everything*. Outside is everything that is not inside. The entirety of the ever-expanding cosmos is outside your skin. And since there can be no inside without an outside, they are as one.

Inside and outside exist together.

I am not *part* of the universe. I *am* the universe. I am.

And yet, I crave purpose.

Why?

Theodore Roosevelt said, "Far and away the best prize that life has to offer is the chance to work hard at work worth doing." That may not be spiritual advice, but it's certainly presidential. And not without insight. Work equals purpose. Said the master to the slave.

What, then, is purpose?

Isn't the desire for purpose nothing more than envy? Charlie Munger said, "The world is not driven by greed. It's driven by envy."

Stay with me, and I think you'll see my point. To want a purpose in life is seen as borderline altruistic. If you desire purpose, you have ambition—either spiritually or materially. And we all think that's fine. But when we see someone with a higher purpose, a higher calling, we perceive that someone's purpose as better than our own. If you believe your purpose is to provide for your family, and you set down that path, and you succeed in providing your family with a solid, comfortable, upper-middle-class American life—then you've fulfilled your purpose. If you notice your neighbor has done better, made a bit more money, bought finer cars, upgraded to a grander house, sent his children to ivy-league schools while your children attend community college—don't you then feel less-than? Doesn't your purpose then fall short? Don't you then feel envious, and think to yourself, my purpose must be more than this. What is my true purpose? And over again it starts. If you are a surgeon that saves a hundred lives, and your colleague has saved a thousand…

You're envious. We compare ourselves to others. As Charles Kindleberger put it, "There is nothing so disturbing to one's well-being and judgment as to see a friend get rich."

Munger and Kindleberger (businessmen) were talking about money when they spoke of envy, but they've seen through to a deeper, more universal truth. J. Krishnamurti—hailed by the Dalai Lama as "One of the greatest thinkers of our age"—has addressed envy, saying that we are forever measuring what we are against what we should be. Comparing ourselves to others, he says, "Is one of the primary causes of conflict." In his talks,

Krishnamurti revisits the topic often, going so far as to say that all organized religions (and society itself) are built on envy.

Even if you discover your purpose and live your purpose and manifest your purpose, it will never be enough. There will always be someone else manifesting their purpose on a higher plane than you.

Despite living in the age of participation trophies, the best prize can only be awarded to one person.

So, if the best prize that life has to offer is the chance to work hard at work worth doing, what is worth doing?

The sacred act of murder?

The Divine Game

LILA IS THE HINDU CONCEPT OF THE UNIVERSE AS A PLAYGROUND of the divine. A game that God plays. And in this game, individual life forms are of no hierarchal importance. An amoeba does not rank above a human. We will live and die our biological lives, just as a strand of seaweed might live and die—in the blink of the cosmic eye.

All that exists, *is*. It has being. If it helps, you could consider this *being* as the essence of God. To one degree or another, all that exists has the spark of God. Therefore, everything—*everything*—is alive. Even a rock. All of us—a rock, a strand of seaweed, a human—are alive. Not a part of or apart from the universe, but rather we *are* the universe. We are the playground of the divine.

Most religions have some kernel of this idea. Hindus not only believe all life goes through birth, life, death, and rebirth, but that all living things have an atman, which is another way of saying God-essence or soul.

And yet, as Eckhart Tolle tells us, we only know ourselves as form (body and thought). We do not know our eternal selves. Our atman. We do not realize that the game goes on forever. It always has gone on. It always will go on. It is now. But we don't perceive this, so we live in fear and suffering. Fear of impermanence. Fear of the inevitable dissolution of our thoughts and bodies. And yet we exist forever. We have always existed, and we always will exist.

It's a divine game. A play.

When we do experience the spiritual awakening, by becoming the witness of our own thoughts, by observing the observer, we join the realm of God. We can sit back and enjoy the game. Enjoy the play. Life is lighthearted, not meant to be taken so seriously. This is why we laugh when someone slips on a banana peel. This is why we guffaw when we witness someone split their pants or stumble and fall on the dance floor. We watch endless videos of our fellow humans failing spectacularly. And we laugh. We are entertained. Just as God is entertained by the misery that befalls each of us.

VIVIEN, AFTER

Observe the observer. Awaken into your presence and relish the divine game. Once awakened, you no longer identify with form (your body, your thoughts). You enjoy the game and witness the glorious, eternal play.

And since our biological lives exist as form (a form we no longer identify with when we become the observer) what better prize than to help others see that they are not only part of the universe, but they actually *are* the universe. Inseparable from it.

Assist them to disidentify with physical forms and thought forms. Extinguish the biological, so that their pure consciousness (the part of us that is eternal, not the impermanent physical manifestation) may enjoy the play, watch the game.

Set them free from the anguish and suffering of earthly manifestation, from this illusion of separate form.

Everything that exists, has always existed, and always will exist.

Murder and Other So-Called Misdeeds

Conversely, whether murder (and other so-called misdeeds) is reasonable—an act of kindness or lighthearted fun, not meant to be taken so seriously—is almost beside the point. If another human being bothers you—impedes your game play by disrupting your presence—you have two choices. Accept what is or take action to change it.

You can identify what may be impeding you by monitoring your internal monologue. Bear witness to those thoughts generated by your mind. Not your purposeful thoughts. Thought borne of purpose is always beneficial. Rather, monitor your unconscious thoughts, that internal monologue, the voice that comes unbidden and never ceases. Listen to *those* thoughts. Stand outside yourself, observe your mind-generated thoughts not born of purpose. The background static. Observe these unbidden thoughts, but don't judge.

Are you complaining? Are your thoughts a repetitive replay of the wrongs perpetrated against you by your fellow man? Do your thoughts consist of daydreams of the things you should have said in a certain situation? These are thoughts of the past. The past does not exist. You cannot return to the past and change it. How can you change what does not exist?

Are you daydreaming of the things you might say the next time you see that person who wronged you? You are thinking of the future. The future does not exist.

The past does not exist. The future does not exist. Only the now exists.

When you dwell on the past or the future, you make yourself either the victim or the hero. In either case, you refute the now. You resist the present moment, and the present moment is all you have ever had and all you will ever have. So why are you resisting it?

Oh, but you say, my present life is miserable. I hate my life. Again, you resist the present moment. Rather than ruminate on how your past mistakes got you to this present moment, or how some dreamed-of person or thing will deliver you to a fulfilled (and nonexistent) future, accept the present moment. And, as I said, if your current life circumstance (your now) is unacceptable, then take action to change your situation. Or don't.

Either change or don't change. If you choose to not change, because it would just be too hard, then accept that you've chosen to accept. You are no longer denying the now. You are no longer living an unconscious life. You are awake and aware.

Observe your complaining thoughts. Smile at them. They have no power over you—you, the observer of those thoughts.

The past is dead. It never existed. Now is the only thing that has ever existed, the only thing that ever will exist. We do not end at our skin. We are what is inside and what is outside. Outside is mostly space. We are eternal. Only a few highly evolved humans have seen this truth. Jesus Christ saw it. Buddha saw it. Oppenheimer saw it.

Van Gogh saw it. Gazing outside the asylum window. The swirling nighttime sky. The universe ceaselessly expanding. *The stars. My God, the stars*.

Faulkner saw it. The past is never dead, he wrote. It's not even past.

How could it be?

Disidentification

ACCORDING TO MANY POPULAR SPIRITUAL TEACHERS, enlightenment happens in a flash for a lucky few. A spiritual epiphany. All at once you see it. You see the universe as God-essence. You see that the deeper you (the presence that observes your thoughts), is divinely created. You yourself are God-essence. But for most of us it's a process. A journey.

The ignition of that process is disidentification from your thoughts. Your thoughts are not you.

As I said, for a lucky few, this comes as a sudden realization, but for others, like me, it is a process. We must wait for lapses in our internal monologues. A pause in that ceaseless, repetitive chatter. Then latch on to that silence, that stillness, and widen the gap, because it's in that gap that your true self exists.

But how do you get there? How do you find those pauses?

When you are the observer of your thoughts, *you* (your presence, your pure consciousness, your God-spark) can simply watch like an audience-member at a play. Mr. Eckhart Tolle suggests we might be amused by our minds and learn not take those mind-created thoughts so seriously. We can chuckle at our observed thoughts as we would at the rambunctious misdeeds of a naughty toddler. After all, what is murder, incest, slavery, genital mutilation, misogyny, torture, fratricide, and infanticide to God? It's light entertainment. Have you read the Old Testament? Have you read Shakespeare? These are the toys that litter the playground of being. Misanthropy, murder, theft, adultery, greed, perversion, abomination after abomination—the props scattered on the stage of the human drama. And yes, kindness, charity, devotion, regard, humility, etc.—less used, a bit dusty.

But I've gotten away from the point. When you observe your mind (rather than identify with your mind—your thoughts are not you), you can see those pauses quite clearly. And then observe what is there. What is present when your mind isn't thinking?

The eternal you.

Your thoughts are not *you*. Your mind is biological and therefore temporary, but *you* are eternal. So, listen to that voice in your head. Watch it. Observe it. But not with anxious concern. And certainly not with judgement. Neither approve nor denounce. Simply observe.

Listen, observe, and wait for pauses. It's during those moments of no-thought (I think of it as the reptilian mind) that you are holy. Those moments when you have disengaged from the mind—seize those moments. And they will happen more often and last longer. These are the moments hard sought by practitioners of meditation.

This is the path to enlightenment. The path to liberation from slavery to the mind.

It seems unattainable, I know. But like all journeys, it starts with but one step.

Watch that internal monologue. Become aware of it. Observe the observer. Bear witness and realize those thoughts are not you.

The End of ME

IS IT POSSIBLE TO COMPLETELY EMPTY THE MIND OF THE *ME*? AND why would we want to do such a thing? Why would we desire a mind devoid of the me?

I am me. Why would I rid myself of me?

Because the me carries quite a bit of unwelcome baggage with it. Learning. Conditioning. Past experiences. Prejudices. That sort of thing. The stuff that prevents you from actually *seeing*. How can you observe if you can't see? In order to truly see, to see without the veil of prejudice or societal norms or the weight of the perceived past, you must rid your mind of the me.

Let's say, for instance, the observing mind retains a sense of right and wrong—morality—then the observer's observations are necessarily tainted by that morality. Do you understand what I'm getting at? A conditioned mind (and the me is most certainly a conditioned mind) cannot witness without judging or intellectualizing or labeling.

In order to truly see, we must rid the mind of the me. What's left in the absence of the me is simply the mind, which, like a clear mountain lake, reflects an image without giving thought to that image.

So, then, is it possible to completely empty the mind of the me?

According to Indian philosopher Jiddu Krishnamurti, it is entirely possible. The me can be eradicated at both the conscious and the deeply unconscious level. But, he said, there is no process or method to rid the mind of me.

It isn't something that can be done through meditation, or self-hypnosis, or asceticism, or any of that silliness.

It can't be done gradually.

It must be done instantly.

Observe the Observer
(*When I's Dead and Gone*)

VIVIEN WILLIAMS ALWAYS RANG TWICE.

Two short rings to announce her intention—no delay to await a response—then she walked into her sister's home. Middle class. No props on display.

Unless you counted Clift Briggs, Vivien's nephew. Clift was the stuff of melodrama. Clift was in the living room reclined in his custom-fitted wheelchair. Vivien's sister, Liz, walked in, towing an invisible cloud of soft perfume, her head angled as she put on an earring.

"We won't be long."

"Where's Bruce?"

"In the car. Waiting. Irritated."

Vivien walked over to Clift and touched his arm so he would know she was in the room with him. He likely already knew Vivien was present. He had probably felt the sound waves when Vivien rang the doorbell twice. If not, he would have smelled her unique scent—not as blatant as Liz's perfume, but distinct, nonetheless.

Clift was deaf and blind. Deafblind was the correct terminology, but Vivien found that term, *deafblind*, to be a bit blunt. In your face. Clift was twenty-three now, fully grown, but he had experienced oxygen deprivation at birth which caused cerebral palsy and sensory loss. Cognitive ability was impacted to an unknown degree. The CP also resulted in spastic quadriplegia. It affected the muscles of his legs, arms, and trunk—leaving Clift with stiff, jerky, awkward movements. Spasticity.

Clift could not walk, talk, see, or hear.

Vivien and Liz were named after Vivien Leigh and Elizabeth Taylor. Old Hollywood. So, Liz and her ex-husband had named their son after the method actor, Montgomery Clift.

VIVIEN, AFTER

Liz once joked that they should have named him Tommy. Like the deaf, dumb, and blind kid who sure played mean pinball. Then she started crying.

The crying days were over. Liz had long ago accepted that, "it is what it is."

Looking at herself in the foyer mirror, Liz said, "He still needs to eat." Vivien glanced at the table tray attached to the arms of the wheelchair and saw three jars of baby food, a plastic bowl of pureed hot dogs, and a rubber-tipped feeding spoon.

Clift wore his standard attire—sweatpants and a sweatshirt. No underwear or t-shirt underneath. Clift was continent, had control of his bladder and bowel, and indicated when he needed to relieve himself by making his hand into a fist, with the thumb poking out between the bent index and middle fingers. The ASL sign *T* for toilet. But he still required assistance to get his pants down and the bedpan or urinal in place. He didn't weigh much, so sometimes it was easier to scoop him up and place him on the accessible toilet seat. In either case, underwear made it more of a chore. And if he accidentally wetted or soiled his clothing, sweats were easy to get on and off.

Vivien said, "I've got it," as she sat down at Clift's powerchair and pried the top off a jar of Puréed carrots. The lid came off with the satisfying pop of the vacuum seal breaking. This made Vivien think of the vast vacuum of space. Vaster than the human mind was capable of conceiving. She knew the observable Universe was 92 billion light-years in diameter, and 95% of that was space.

Empty space.

We are mostly empty space.

Not only was a single human life insignificant in the face of 92 billion light-years (and ceaselessly expanding), but our tiny little planet was also insignificant. Carl Sagan famously called it the pale blue dot. In 1977, NASA launched Voyager 1, a space probe programmed to seek the outer Solar System beyond our sun's heliosphere. In 1990, as Voyager 1 was reaching the threshold of our solar system, Sagan suggested the camera look back for a moment, instead of ever forward. The resulting image (taken from 4 billion miles away—0.000680431180093 light years) showed our planet as nothing more than a wanly illuminated speck of dust—a pale blue dot—less than a pixel in size.

Sagan urged that we consider that pale blue dot. "That's home. That's us," he said. "On it everyone you love, everyone you know, everyone you ever heard of, every human being who ever was, lived out their lives. The aggregate of our joy and suffering, thousands of confident religions, ideologies, and economic doctrines, every hunter and forager, every hero and coward, every creator and destroyer of civilization, every king and peasant, every young couple in love, every mother and father, hopeful child,

VIVIEN, AFTER

inventor and explorer, every teacher of morals, every corrupt politician, every "superstar," every "supreme leader," every saint and sinner in the history of our species lived there--on a mote of dust suspended in a sunbeam."

And here Vivien was, on a mote of dust suspended in a sunbeam, spooning pureed hotdog into the salivating mouth of her deafblind nephew.

Liz double-checked her wallet, about to leave. Vivien called out, "Does Bruce have the keys to the lift van? We might go out for a nature hike later. Get some fresh air."

"They're hanging up. Thanks so much."

"Okay. See you later."

Vivien scraped the last bits of carrot, beans, and applesauce into a single spoonful and offered it to her nephew by tapping the spoon on his chin, but he burped lightly and turned his head away. Finished.

Clift waved his T fist in the air. Vivien glanced down at the young man's lap and saw that he knew his mother had just left. And he knew exactly who was here feeding him. He'd known it from the first second of the first minute Vivien had walked in.

She wiped his chin and pulled down his sweatpants.

A Very Simple Philosophy

THE SUN HAD BEGUN ITS DESCENT, A YELLOW-ORANGE BLOB sliding down the hard blue wall of sky.

They were at the Kennesaw Mountain Park. The Kennesaw Mountain National Battlefield Park. Suburban joggers mixed with hikers and dog-walkers and mountain bikers and videographers—all out to get a little fresh air and take selfies on a three-thousand-acre tract of land where multitudes of young men had died as the South tried fruitlessly to stem William Sherman's march to Atlanta. Vivien thought it highly unlikely any of those boys defending the right to own human chattel were aware of their true selves. That they were present. Awakened. In the Now. She likewise doubted General Sherman was in a state of enlightenment.

She knew Clift couldn't see the mountain or the green-patinaed canons, or the protruding obelisk monument to the Confederate dead, but he could smell the honeysuckle, the mimosa blooms, the dank creek water. He could feel the exposed tree roots that rocked his chair. Feel last season's pine needles rain down on his face in the strong breeze. Perhaps he could feel the God-essence of the human beings who had ended their biological lives here. Or simply the God-essence of the mountain itself.

Peering down from a graying wood-slat bridge, Vivien watched the scummy dark surface of a slow-moving creek. Just a dark streak of water surrounded by a mudflat plain. She searched the cloudy water, staring, gazing, witnessing. Looking for what? Serenity? Enlightenment? Bliss? You can't find enlightenment by looking for it. You can't attain enlightenment by desiring to attain enlightenment. You can't get it by desiring it. And you can't desire to stop desiring. So, what is there to do? Be still. Still your thoughts. Still your Self. Think no-thoughts. Allow the reptilian brain to arise.

That's when she noticed tiny ripples on the membranous surface of the water. Water that had appeared devoid of life only moments before. In her stillness, she saw a ripple. A ripple here, a ripple there. Echoing. She could see tiny insects in the water. Her reptilian brain sent a signal to dart out her tongue. To slither it forward, seeking food to feed the brain. In resisting that impulse, Vivien lost the connection, lost her stillness. Nonetheless, her awareness had been awakened, so she observed.

Ripples. On the surface of the water. Made by insects so slender and spindly, so lightweight, they stood on top of the water. They were water striders. Their bodies weren't substantial enough to disrupt the surface tension. They walked on water. Like Jesus. She couldn't remember ever learning about water striders, but she must have, at some point in her life. How else could she know what they were called? How could she know that they communicated with each other by tapping the surface of the water with their feet, creating capillary waves that other water striders sense using motion-detecting cilia on their legs.

How could she know that? More importantly, what were they saying to each other? What was the urgent communique? That all water striders are created equal?

A series of ripples blinked on and off—onetwothreefourfivesix—in rapid succession. They must have something important to say to each other. The capillary waves looked like little bombs going off. Like the blast waves of tiny atom bombs. Like global thermonuclear warfare, writ miniature.

Onetwothreefourfivesix. She could imagine the lilliputian, doomlike percussion of each warhead.

As she watched, she realized that in addition to the water striders and their ripples, she could see her own reflection in the water. In silhouette, the sun a post-impressionistic orb of apple jelly behind her. But it was her. She knew Alan Watts had spoken of a Zen poem by Chuang-tzu: *The perfect man employs his mind as a mirror; it grasps nothing; it refuses nothing; it receives but does not keep.*

Watts compared this to wild geese that fly over water with no intent to cast their reflection. And the water has no mind to retain their image. The lake had no *me*.

And she realized she was literally observing the observer. She was witness to her own thoughts. Witness to her thoughts, witness to her physical self and witness to the water striders. She had mind to retain the reflection, but the water did not. What did that mean? What was she supposed to do with this knowledge? Was the point not to retain it? Grasp nothing, refuse nothing, receive but not keep? Or was a mirror just another prop on the stage God had dressed for us?

What did it mean to witness?

This made her wonder who else was witnessing this. She imagined an intelligence gazing down on our planet, as we waged nuclear Armageddon on ourselves. To that intelligence, the explosions might appear as tiny capillary waves. Ripples of energy across the planet's surface. And the alien observer might think, *oh, look at those lifeforms who live on this planet. They stride across the surface. And those energy waves, that's how they communicate with each other. They tap the surface of the globe, creating ripples the others can sense with cilia on their legs. Oh, look, onetwothreefourfivesix! They must have something important to say to each other.*

Vivien understood the water-strider-ripples were energy waves. Just as our voices are energy waves. Just as our thoughts are energy waves. And she realized, energy never dies. Energy can neither be created nor destroyed. The law of conservation of energy—the first law of thermodynamics—states that the energy of a closed system must remain constant. It can neither increase nor decrease without interference from outside. The universe itself is a closed system, so the total amount of energy in existence has always been the same. The forms that energy takes, however, are always changing.

So those ripples the water striders made went on forever. For eternity. Just like our thoughts and our words and our deeds and the energy of life itself. We are eternal. We can never truly die.

So, she could never truly kill someone.

Eternity is a long time. She watched the ripples flash on and off, like SOS signals. Morse code. Or thermonuclear warfare. Communications she could never understand. The wave of each ripple dissipating, growing ever smaller, smaller beyond her capacity to comprehend, yet nonetheless going on forever.

•••

She watched the last ripple dissipate before turning away, so that she and Clift might continue their journey. She wondered, what if, for each water strider, each never-truly-dissipating ripple was the end of the first second, of the first minute, of the first hour, of their first day in hell. What then?

Finally on their way, Vivien thought of the law of attraction. We draw what we need to us. But also, alarmingly, we draw to us that which we fear—merely by fearing it. We see the thing that most horrifies us, and we become that very thing. It was all so clear now. What we fear most is what we ultimately manifest in our lives. That is the law of attraction. Darkness is drawn to darkness. Darkness is not drawn to light. It is divided by the light, and drawn to itself. It is repelled by the light. It is one and the same as the light. Darkness cannot exist without light. Two sides of the same coin. They can never touch but are inseparable. Darkness is drawn to darkness, and light is drawn to light.

She was living in the present, not the past, not the future, but the Now. All her awareness was focused on now. And she wondered, was it perhaps possible, that right now—this present moment—was the beginning of her first second, of her first minute, of her first hour, of her first day in hell?

And what of Clift? Was he in hell? Did he desire an end to suffering? Did he desire death so that he might be reborn in a more acceptable form?

She had this thought, but by then her moment of awareness had passed. She was no longer in the present, no longer the witness to her own thoughts. She was thinking of the future.

The Web and the Rock

ALONG THE WOODED PATH THEY JOURNEYED. THEY PASSED A man and woman filming themselves perched on a resurrected civil war canon. Clift used a joystick control to propel his motorized wheelchair. At home, where the layout was familiar—memorized—orientation and mobility were not a problem. Out here, Vivien used a bit of string—one end tied to her wrist, the other to Clift's—so he could safely follow yet independently move. The path wasn't wheelchair friendly. Exposed roots and protruding stones caused his chair to rock violently at times.

They had left the dark mirror of the creek behind. What use of a mirror had Clift? What use of a mirror had she? A mirror was a boring prop. It was *Sleeping Beauty* stuff. Yes, a mirror was symbolically potent, but it was just a word, and words were merely symbols for ideas. Props were tools to act out those ideas.

Misanthropy, adultery, greed, perversion, incest, slavery, mutilation, misogyny, torture.

Props. Just props.

Murder.

If she wanted to, Vivien could lead her nephew over a mountain drop-off (push Clift over a cliff), or bash his head with a rock, or push him into stagnant water and sucking mud. She could tip him over into the mudflats and watch him slowly sink. The powerchair was easily 200 pounds.

Clift ran over a chunk of black-and-white striped granite. The reverberation almost rocked him from the chair. Vivien stopped. The rock was mostly buried but looked to be about the size of a bowling ball.

She signed into Clift's hand so he would be expecting it.

It took a few minutes of exertion to free the rock from the earth's grip. She worked it to-and-fro, breaking a nail. But it came out of the ground, and she hefted it up. She looked around to make sure there were no observers observing the observer and held the heavy rock to the sky, high above Clift's fragile head. She had a memory of a memory, a flash of the collective unconscious, of a distant primitive ancestor—a dark player—holding this same rock, picking up this same stage prop, and bashing out the brains of a foe—or a disabled family member slowing the tribe down, and therefore better off dead. A mercy killing. Or killing for no reason at all. Killing simply for the sake of killing.

As gently as possible, Vivien set the rock in Clift's lap. He grinned and made a howling sound of surprise and pleasure at the immense weight now born by his spindly legs. His body jerked in pleasure, spastic and lacking control. This went on until he regained some small amount of restraint over his limbs and allowed his hands to play over the rough surface of what had almost thrown him from his chair—the way a serpent may cause a horse to throw its rider.

Vivien thought about the green-tinged halo of darkly glistening mud that edged the creek. Right down the hill. A short, bumpy wheelchair-shove away. She thought of the sucking mud, engorging itself on the boy and the stone and the powerchair, engulfing them the same way the unhinged jaw of a boa constrictor allows the snake to engulf a mouse, pulling it in slowly, impossibly.

She thought of time. Decamillennia. The wink of an eye in the face of eternity. She thought of paleobiologists, eons from now, chipping away at the fossilized mud, sifting through sand and rock debris, long dead algae and lower aquatic life forms, hoping for an antediluvian footprint, and finding the mineralized outlines of feathers, ferns, and Clift.

They kept moving. Clift balanced the granite rock in his lap. Vivien nudged him to stop. They had come to a sweetgum tree. It was old, gnarled, near death. Close to the time of dissolution that all life forms must face. There was a knothole in the tree, a cavity, and it made Vivien think of the knothole in the oak tree in *To Kill a Mockingbird*. The recluse Boo Radley left presents there for Jem and Scout.

This knothole passed through the center of the tree, and it was open at both sides of the bole. The setting sun filtered through the opening, so that on Vivien's side, the east, the opening had an amber glow. Ethereal. Eldritch. The knothole was dark and forbidding, but the dappled sun cast wanly through, illuminating a spider's web inside. It was not a traditional web design, not a spiral orb, but a chaotic, multi-layered, three-dimensional diorama. It looked tangled, with a purpose that could be sensed but not defined. Like the universe. Purposeful chaos. The web was a universe unto itself.

But there were no presents hidden in this dark nebula. No sticks of gum or old coins, or soap-bar carvings. She knew what was in the knothole. She recognized the tangled silk. It was a black widow's web. A universe of one. A universe upon which she dared not intrude.

She signed into Clift's palm.

Trust me?

He grinned and his body rocked with excitement.

Yes.

Vivien reached forward and toggled the joystick controller until she had navigated the chair alongside the tree. She took Clift's hand, signing once again into the open palm.

Trust me. Don't tell.

And guided his hand into the dark hole.

Abomination

BLACK WIDOWS ONLY BITE WHEN THEY'RE FORCED. WHEN GIVEN no alternative. When pressed or squeezed. As when trapped in a shoe by an invading foot. Confined, they bite.

Clift had not been bitten. A handful of sticky webbing was the only price either of them had to pay for what was quite a thrill. The universe is all about thrills. Ask Alan Watts. Of course, it had cost that black widow her entire world, but she could build another.

Along they went, away from the creek, the web in tatters, the rock discarded on the ground—a bit of stage dressing, to be picked up by the next dark player who might find such a prop of use in telling their story. Perhaps someone might pick it up in a fit of self-righteous rage and crack their lover's skull. Or perhaps someone might catch their foot on it and take a tumble. A pratfall. Break their arm. Greenstick fracture. The universe would find it comical. The universe would find either scenario entertaining. It could happen tomorrow or ten billion years from now.

It's all the same to the universe.

They came to a fork where the way diverged into a less-used trail that veered off from the main path. It was more of a deer trail, barely discernable, obscured by evergreens, but it bore an even surface carpeted smooth with brown pine needles. Vivien hesitated a moment. In the long run, she knew, there was still time to change the path she was on. She contemplated, then held back the overgrowth and led Clift deeper into the woods. Deeper. Deeper. She chose the path less travelled by, and that choice made all the difference.

After a while, they came to a place where the ground was barren. Exposed rock. She could see ripples in the rock from when it had once been lava. From when these mountains had formed. Seeing the ripples in the rock was like seeing chalk plumb lines on stage set construction. Evidence that this world was not real, but rather had been built. Specially constructed. It was Trompe-l'œil.

No trees could take root in the bare rock, so the sky was open, and the last of the sunlight came down like a weak spotlight. Thus illuminated, they stopped.

It was quiet. Still. She could hear hikers, muffled laughter off in the distance, carried to them by the mountain arena. But they were alone. Observed, as far as she knew, only by the divine, and perhaps the unseeing eyes of long dead soldiers.

Vivien signed into her nephew's hand.

Secret.

Don't tell.

Our secret.

He grinned and his body contracted in glee.

Vivien massaged his arms, legs, torso, calming the spasticity. She took off his shirt, massaging. Clift lifted his hips obligingly as she tugged down his pants.

With the ghosts of the Confederate dead watching, she straddled the chair. It was like breaking a wild horse. She didn't think it was going to happen. But it did.

And she looked down at him after. He was shivering in the warm sun. Shivering, shriveling.

Vivien thought: *Abomination.*

And the witnessing-self realized that the word *abomination* was just that—a word. Sometimes words have two meanings. But always, always, a word is a symbol. A label. A symbolic representation of something that may or may not be real. A judgement born of mind conditioning.

All words are symbols.

A Hole in the Earth and a Vessel in the Sky

H E WASN'T READING FROM THE BIBLE. AS SPIRITUAL LEADER TO a community that often found itself in turmoil, in need of a deeper relationship with Christ, Vivien's husband knew the scriptures cold. KJV, ASV, NIV, HCSB—William Williams knew them all.

"His mother and brothers waited outside to see Him. To talk to Him. A crowd gathered around Jesus, surrounding Him, and the crowd said, 'Your mother and Your brothers are outside, seeking You. They want to talk to You.' Jesus's response—to our modern ears, to our human way of thinking—was quite odd, perhaps even cold. He said, 'Who is my mother and who are my brothers?' Looking at those who were sitting in a circle around him, He said, 'Here is my mother. Here are my brothers. For whoever does the will of my father in heaven, that person is my brother and sister and mother.'

"Do you hear that, mother, brother, sister? Do you have ears to hear? Can you listen and accept those words still today? Do you hear His voice? The significance. The deeper clarity. Listen to His words that reverberate across the millennia. Whoever does the will of God is brother to Jesus, sister to Jesus, and mother to Jesus. *Mother to Jesus*. Think of it. All of you life-givers, look here. Mothers, look here at the cross behind me. Do you see it? Where they drove the iron nails—deeper, deeper, and deeper with each blow. So sweet. So sweet. A sweet, simple sacrifice. Look right here over my shoulder. *Here*. Right here."

He pointed to the cross.

"Woman, here is your son."

Wow. Vivien was impressed. That was quite powerful. And improvised.

"If you take one message home with you this Mother's Day Sunday, one idea, one word, it's *echoes*. Everything you do in this life echoes. It goes on forever. So, make a promise to yourself. Make a promise to make a noise. Start something that will echo forever, through space and time. Through Heaven and earth."

VIVIEN, AFTER

From the pulpit, Pastor Williams paused and cleared his throat. "Do you know who else started an echo? Made a noise? Jesus Christ. Jesus Christ. Jesus Christ. So sweet the sacrifice. So sweet the means of death. That sacrifice, that death and resurrection, still echo today. Deeper, perhaps, than ever before. It will echo forever. We are His sheep, and He is the Good Shepherd. He died for us. He died voluntarily. For his sheep. For us. He said, 'I am laying down my life so I may take it up again. No one takes it from me, but I lay it down on my own.'

"So I challenge you to do the same. Lay down your life. In service to Christ. Jesus Christ, your son. Jesus Christ, your brother. Start an echo. Make some noise. I challenge you to rend a hole in the earth and place a vessel in the sky. Do you hear me? You brother-sister, father-mother, aunt-uncle, friend and frienemy."

The last bit didn't even get a chuckle. As always, William had practiced his sermon on Vivien. She was his test audience. Part of her wifely duties. He was concerned *frienemy* was a little too colloquial. A little too cutesy. Not appropriate. Vivien suggested replacing it with the term *shade thrower*. Or *dark player*.

"Dark prayer? What? Seriously?"

"No, dark *player*. Dark player or shade thrower."

"Oh. What do those even mean?"

Vivien shrugged.

William said he was aiming for something a little more messianic. Her ideas were a trifle too satanic.

"In that case," she'd urged him, "keep it as-is." To salvage that paltry bit of levity. His sermons tended toward damnation.

From the pulpit, he thundered, "Rend a hole in the earth and place a vessel in the sky."

William let that hang in the air for a bit. Vivien had no idea what it meant. But it sure sounded good, she had to give him that. It sounded very, very good. It was all in the delivery, that was true, and William was a master of delivery. She had seen him so worked up, so on fire with the Holy Spirit, that his face purpled, and a rope of foam-flecked saliva leapt from his mouth and dangled like obscene jewelry from his over-shaved chin.

"Yes." Much quieter now. A whisper. "A hole in the earth and a vessel in the sky."

It was poetry. But he needed to tie it all together, get it over with. So these good people of the community could get home to their SSRIs. To their DoorDash and pork roasts and marshmallow salads. So the tithes could be counted, and Vivien could go home and read and then go out to Golden Corral for dinner and have Christ-approved, Aqua-Velva-fogged relations with her husband. A thrill. We all wanted a thrill.

"And what shall you bury in this hole? What might issue forth from this vessel in the sky?"

VIVIEN, AFTER

He gave them a solid thirty-seconds to come up with their own answer before supplying them with the conclusion he wanted them to draw.

"Echoes. Ripples. A single act of kindness. Be a brother to somebody. Be a mother to the motherless. We all need mothers. Your actions will echo. An act of charity will ripple. Tell your coworker about Jesus Christ. Maybe he or she hasn't heard the Word, has not yet accepted the Living God. Share the Word. Start an echo. Watch it ripple. That homeless man you see every day on the highway exit ramp. The one holding up a sign. A message written on a tattered piece of cardboard. That message was written just for you. Don't ignore it. God wrote that sign. Stop. Read it. That man is created in the image of God. That man is a child of God. Stop and read His sign. Consider it. God wrote it for you. I urge you to act on those words. Start an echo. A ripple.

"And consider this: When you drive past that homeless man holding up his crudely made sign, those words may be written in a forgotten language. It might look like English to you, but it could be Greek, Latin, Hebrew. You don't know what those words mean. Not really. But they are for you and you alone. So consider them carefully. Find the deeper meaning.

"Jesus, too, had a crude sign tacked onto his cross. A mockery. *Jesus of Nazareth King of the Jews*. Written in Greek, Latin, and Hebrew. For clarity. He hung there, belittled and befouled, spat-upon, scourged, bearing our sins in his body on a tree. In those final moments, dying in agony, Christ spoke. He said, 'Woman, here is your son.'

"He acknowledged that a child needs a mother, and a mother needs a child. Because like newborn babies, we crave pure spiritual milk."

William closed his Bible even though he hadn't been reading from it.

"I command you. Lay down your life. Rend a hole in the earth. And place a vessel in the sky."

The Sacred Stillness of the Present Moment

"I DON'T LOVE YOU ANYMORE AND I DON'T BELIEVE IN GOD."

"You *what?*" He was naked, fresh from the shower, a towel wrapped around his middle. William still had a good body. She admired that about him.

"I don't know how else to say it, so I'm just saying it."

"I knew you were different. Something has influenced you. This is not *you* talking. Something is speaking through you. Is it those books?"

"What books?"

He crossed to her side of the king-size mattress and opened her bedside drawer. He scooped out the books. Trade paperbacks. And cast them onto the bed.

"Eckhart Tolle. Alan Watts. Deepak Chopra. Sadhguru. Why's he sad?" William picked out one book and held it up like a lawyer presenting the murder weapon to jurors. The cover depicted an Indian man with crisp white hair, in profile, head bowed in contemplation. "J. Krishnamurti. *Krishnamurti*? Come on, Vivien." He tossed the book back down. "I don't know that the *J* stands for, but I know what it doesn't stand for. It doesn't stand for Jesus. These books are not Christ-centered."

"No, no they're not. But Christ's name and Christ's words are in there. Along with the Buddha, along with—"

"The Buddha? *The Buddha*? You have got to be kidding. We are Christians, Viv. *Christians*. I am a preacher. I lead a community in devotion to Christ. You didn't buy these in public, did you?"

They existed in the stillness. No past, no future. They existed in the sacred stillness of the present moment.

Breaking the stillness, creating a ripple, William brought up an old score that had yet to be settled. "You're the wife of a Baptist preacher, and you've never been baptized."

"You know I was baptized."

"Lutheran. As a baby. *Sprinkled*. Your head was sprinkled. We do not believe in infant baptism. Baptism is a public declaration of faith and commitment to Jesus Christ—which an infant cannot do. An infant is incapable of making that choice. And we don't sprinkle. We don't drip and pour. You know that. We immerse. We believe in immersion. Immersion *below* the surface and *into* the water. We don't fling droplets. We don't lightly wet. Full immersion. That's what the word *baptism* means."

"I understand English. The word "baptism" describes the action of dipping or plunging something. Our English word "baptize" comes from a Greek word that means "to dip" or "immerse."

"I know you know that. I didn't mean anything by it. Baptism, specifically meaning immersion, is more of a southern Baptist idiom."

"Regardless, it's only symbolic."

"Of course it's symbolic. Death. Burial. Resurrection. Only a submerged body can represent death—a burial of the old self. Only emerging out of the water can represent resurrection—a new life."

"You may not quite understand what the word *symbolic* means. Immersion, affusion, aspersion. It all amounts to the same thing. It all symbolizes the same thing. You say *tomato*, and I say *tomahto*."

"Viv."

"Everybody assumes I've been baptized. Dunked. Let it go. With you it's always water, water, water. It's primitive. Just drag me into the backyard and plunge me into the creek. Seriously. Right now. This instant. Now is the acceptable time."

"It has to be public. It's a public profession of faith."

"The birds can watch. There's a songbird."

"There's a what?"

"On a tree. By the brook. A songbird who sings sometimes. It sings to me. My head hums with it."

"That branch water is polluted, Vivien. You know that. It's a foul and filthy ditch."

"That makes it perfect for me."

"Viv, you're not well. Honestly, you're not okay."

"No, I'm not okay. I've never been okay. I never will be okay. I don't love you anymore and I don't believe in God. Not your hydrophilic God. Not your narrow definition of God. I want a divorce."

He gaped. She knew he could live with her difference. Her crisis of faith. Her evolution of faith. He could live with her atheism or paganism or Hinduism or Wiccan rites. Her submerged self or her sprinkled self. He could live with any of that. Those were private affairs. But divorce was public.

"'What therefore God hath joined together, let not man put asunder.' Those are the words of Jesus Christ. They are printed in red ink, Vivien. *Red ink*. Are those words in those books? We can't get divorced."

"Yes, we can."

"No. We can work this out. I act as marriage counselor for these families. I can't be divorced. I would rather be widowed."

Widowed. It made her think of the black widow, existing in the sacred stillness of its universe constructed of self.

"I would rather die myself than see our marriage die. We can't be divorced. It's bad enough we don't have any children. I would rather you die or I die than break our covenant with God. Do you hear me? I'm begging you, Vivien. I would rather die."

She knew William was not self-aware. Not in the present moment. His mind was reeling with thoughts of the future. Fear. He was consumed with fear. She doubted he had ever been fully conscious in his entire life. If he could only step outside himself. Observe his own thoughts.

"I'm going to Liz's. I want you to have this moment to be with yourself."

The Knack and How to Get It

SHE HAD THE KNACK FOR MAKING THINGS HAPPEN IN HER FAVOR. Most of the spiritualists called it synchronicity. She was pretty sure Carl Jung had come up with the theory of synchronicity, but she had never read any Jung and had no plans to do so. It was weird how she had access to knowledge—facts and insights in her mind—that she had no memory of learning. It was as if a different version of Vivien had learned those things, experienced those experiences, and the residual knowledge was at her fingertips whenever she needed it.

Jung defined synchronicity as "meaningful coincidence." Both Watts and Tolle speak of the idea that as we come into alignment with the universe, awake to our true selves and approach enlightenment, we may find that things just happen for us.

Cormac McCarthy—he had the knack. He said he was always lucky. "That's the way my life has been. Just when things were really, really bleak, something would happen."

"Something would always turn up," he said of living in a house in Tennessee without electricity. "I had no money, I mean none. I had run out of toothpaste, and I was wondering what to do when I went to the mailbox and there was a free sample."

That is synchronicity.

Not long after, McCarthy found a MacArthur Fellowship check for $236,000.00 in that same mailbox.

That's the knack.

When suburban housewives say "I haven't seen you in twenty years, but I had a dream about you yesterday, and today here you are. The universe brought you back into my life," or something similar, this is not synchronicity. This isn't the knack. This is most likely confirmation bias. Or just an example of humans seeking meaning in patterns. Seeking meaning in patterns may not even be uniquely human. It may be atavistic. It may be reptilian.

The reptilian complex is the oldest part of the brain—the brainstem and the basal ganglia. This lizard brain is the seat of primordial urges such as hunger, sex, thirst, and greed. It's home to rote habits and so-called muscle memory—like riding a bike.

(Vivien Williams did indeed have the insight that she, herself, was a suburban housewife claiming harmony with the universe. However, the intelligence observing these observations and insights was not Vivien's biological mind (and it certainly wasn't her reptilian brain), but rather the part of her (or more precisely, the *all* of her), that existed in time and space as immortal energy. This Self (this observer of the observer) was one with the universe and understood that the body that hallucinated itself as Vivien Williams was composed of matter. And matter and energy were equivalents. And energy never dies. Energy can neither be created nor destroyed, and therefore Vivien Williams could neither be created nor destroyed. She was neither a spiritualist nor a housewife, but rather both simultaneously.)

Another good example of seeking or inventing patterns is when you look at a clock and the time is 12:34. And the next time you look at the clock, it's 12:34 again. And you make note of this coincidence. You think to yourself, *the last time I looked at the clock, it was 12:34 exactly!* Then, a day or two later, you glance at the time, and my God, it's exactly 12:34. This can't be a coincidence. It's a pattern. The universe must be trying to tell me something.

Well, no, it's not. This imagined pattern feels significant to you because 1234 is a noteworthy number. So, you note it. All the other times you glanced at the clock, and it was 1:45 or 6:21 or 11:16 have been conveniently forgotten. Because those times are mundane. They are not memorable. They are not *noteworthy*. So, you don't take note of them. You immediately forget those times. But 12:34, that's *special*, so it sticks out. You remember it. So that when you glance at the time and it's 12:34 yet again, you think, something is afoot. Somebody or something is trying to tell me something. It could be your dead grandmother trying to communicate with you from beyond the grave. After all, clocks only read 12:34 twice a day, the odds of you just happening to check the time at exactly 12:34 make this more than a coincidence.

What you don't tell yourself is that a clock displays all the other times just twice a day. You might have glanced at the time at exactly 11:16 five days in a row, but it wasn't noteworthy to your pattern-seeking brain. If your grandmother was trying to tell you that you were going to be in a life-altering automobile accident, so please stay home on November sixteenth, and she magically had you look at the time at exactly 11:16 every day for eleven days—it would go right over your head.

This 12:34 pattern perception paradox probably didn't exist in the age of analog clocks, because it's not particularly noteworthy with roman numerals, and, obviously, it is also not an example of the reptilian brain. Lizards can't tell time.

VIVIEN, AFTER

The knack is simply the realization that everything is interconnected and inseparable. Alan Watts said, "Each one of us, not only human beings but every leaf, every weed, exists in the way it does, only because everything else around it does. The individual and the universe are inseparable."

Once you know that, once you understand that you and the universe are inseparable—then you have the knack. Everything breaks for you. Even though you never play the lottery, you may be struck by the impulse to buy a two-dollar scratch-off while you're at the store. And hit for $50,000.00. Or maybe you uncharacteristically exit off the highway during your habitual commute to take the longer way home from work and find out later you narrowly missed a multi-car, multi-fatality accident. These are not coincidences, this is synchronicity. You are inseparable from the universe, and you are synchronized with it.

The universe wants you to have what you want. The universe desires for you to receive what you desire.

Be in tune with the universe. That's how you get the knack.

• • •

Vivien Williams's fervently desired an easy way to get out of her stifling marriage. She knew, per Eckhart Tolle and *The Power of Now*, she had two choices: Either change the situation through action or accept the situation as it was—accept that she had chosen not to change—and find peace through that acceptance and continue her spiritual journey.

The problem was, she didn't like either of those two options.

She desired a different solution.

Her Self observed herself struggling with this problem. Either keep-on-keeping-on or seek a way of ending the marriage that would allow her to continue into enlightenment, but not humiliate or demean her husband.

She decided there was no acceptable solution.

When along came a textbook example of synchronicity.

She desperately wanted release from her marital vows but could think of no acceptable exit strategy.

So, when Vivien's profoundly disabled nephew, Clift Briggs, shot and killed her husband, Pastor William Williams, thereby ending her marriage with no acrimony or embarrassment, Vivien knew this was not a coincidence.

There was no way it could be.

So Sweet the Means of Death

ALAN WATTS TOOK THE ASIAN TEACHINGS OF TAOIST, HINDU, and Buddhist philosophies and popularized them for Western wisdom-seekers. He published more than 25 books and was a habitué of the enlightenment lecture circuit. His books and talks have grown in influence posthumously.

With seven children spread over three marriages, it would be safe to say he had a colorful personal life. We are reminded to separate the teachings from the teacher, and Alan Watts (enlightened and ingloriously human) is the perfect example of this dictum.

Watts was not a guru. He was not a bodhisattva. He was a "philosophical entertainer."

He was enamored of Aldous Huxley's law of reversed effort—the harder we try with the conscious will to do something, the less we shall succeed. For instance, the harder you try to go to sleep, the more you stay awake. The idea is older than Huxley. It's a Daoist concept, and even Jesus expressed it when He said, "For whoever would save his life will lose it."

Echoing Christ, Watts said that if life is what you desire, do not hold onto it. You must let go. Don't cling to it. But how do you let go of what you desire if you desire life? He compared it to an addiction that is likely to end in death. And yet, facing what is in essence suicide, the addict can't give up the habit, "Because the means of death are so sweet."

In his later years, Watts succumbed to alcoholism. He awakened, so to speak, in a bottle. When asked why he drinks so much, Watts reportedly answered "I don't like myself when I'm sober."

It is suggested, but not confirmed, that Alan Watts died by suicide. No one knows for sure exactly how he died. And likely no one ever will know. Because ninety minutes after his death,

VIVIEN, AFTER

Buddhist monks removed Watts's body from his California cabin and cremated the remains in a beachside pyre.

He was 58 years old when he died on Friday, November 16, 1973, at 12:34 a.m.

Ceaseless Chatter

"Just a few questions, Mrs. Williams. I know this is a difficult time."

"My nephew shot and killed my husband in front of three witnesses, detective. What is there to ask? What clarity do you seek?"

"Clarity?"

"Yes, that's generally why we ask questions. To gain clarity. Enlightenment. I seek enlightenment myself."

"Enlightenment. That sounds spiritual."

"I don't know about that. I'm sorry if I don't seem more upset. More bereaved. You have to understand, we were people of faith."

"Were?"

"Well, my husband is dead. He's past tense."

"But you're not past tense, are you? Is your faith past tense? Do you see what I am saying?"

"Faith. That's what I'm getting at. As you well know, my husband was a pastor. A man of faith. So regardless of what you believe or what I believe, or a panhandler on a highway exit ramp..."

"Panhandler?"

"Homeless man. Beggar. Sorry, an *unhoused person*. It's just something he said in a sermon. The point is William believed that those who acknowledge Jesus Christ as the Son of God and accept Him as their personal lord and savior, are truly saved. They are cleansed of sin through Christ's blood. William will dwell in the house of the Lord forever. So, grief is inappropriate. It's a time of celebration."

"Yee-hah."

"Please, sir."

"And you'll join him there? You'll dwell in the house of the Lord forever?"

"I am eternal. As are you."

"That's a lot to take in."

"I can give you a pamphlet."

•••

"Questions. Okay. I don't know. How about for the beginning, where did your nephew get the gun? And for the finish, how did a deaf, blind, and mute kid manage to shoot anybody? Why didn't he just shoot the ceiling? Or the floor? You see what I'm getting at?"

"I believe he did shoot the ceiling. And the floor. And a window. And the wall. And the front door."

"And your husband. He got your husband, too. Right in the heart."

"It was a senseless accident. Clift had no idea what he was doing. That's the tragedy."

"The insurance clouds matter as well."

"Matter?"

"Matters. It clouds matters. The insurance. Do you follow what I am saying, ma'am?"

"Insurance?"

"Yes. The insurance. The life insurance. You follow?"

"Life insurance."

"You didn't know about the life insurance? The policy."

"The policy. No."

"You want to know how much it was for? Since you're just now hearing about it?"

"I... Yes, certainly. I'll need to be informed at some point."

"Since this is a celebration of sorts, let me add to the jubilee."

The detective spoke a number and she knew he was noting the constriction of Vivien Williams's pupils. That he found those eyes to be blank, reptilian. And as he named the dollar amount, those pupils constricted most oddly. They seemed to swirl.

She could see her eyes reflected in his.

"And it has a double indemnity clause."

"I'm not familiar with that term." Of course she was familiar with it. She'd read the book in high school. As a sophomore. "It sounds like a penalty."

"It's not. It's more like a bonus. Extra points. It means the insurance pays double. You follow?"

"Double. My God. Why?"

"You sure you never heard of double indemnity? It's famous. There was a book. You understand?"

"What was the book called?"

"*Double Indemnity.*"

"It seems like there was an old movie."

"Yes, but the book came first. You follow me?"

"Oh."

VIVIEN, AFTER

"Yes. It's a standard thing. When the insured individual dies of accidental causes."

"Oh. Accidental?"

"Yes. Like if they get shot by a deaf, dumb, and blind guy. That would be considered an accident."

"I see."

Vivien glanced at the time. It was 12:34. Her head was humming.

"Yes, an accident. There's no way something like that could be considered purposeful. No one could ever call it manslaughter. Or murder. Of course, whoever gave your nephew the gun, that person would surely be guilty of criminal negligence. Ignoring an obvious risk. Disregarding the life and safety of others."

She lit a cigarette without asking the detective if he minded. It was her house, after all. Her house, her body, her choice. Nobody smoked anymore. It was something she had played with in college before dropping out to marry William. She would never have smoked in front of William—or anybody else for that matter. It was socially unacceptable. And incredibly harmful to the physical self.

She took a long draw, inhaled deeply, and thought, *but the means of death are so sweet*.

"So, naturally, we want to know where Mr. Briggs got the gun. I mean, he didn't drive himself to a pawn shop or a gun show and fill out the paperwork and submit a background check. No waiting period in this state, so he could cash-and-carry. But that never happened. Clift Briggs wouldn't know a Grant from a Benjamin. Are you following what I am saying?"

"I'm sure."

"But that's not the big question, where he got the gun. It's important, and I want to know, but I can think of several scenarios of how Clift Briggs came to be in possession of a .38 special. No, the big question, the one that I absolutely must answer, is what happened to the revolver after the shooting. We got six bullets. He popped them off onetwothreefourfivesix. Bam. You understand, ma'am? Emptied all six chambers. No dry firing. That's according to your statement and the statements of your sister and brother-in-law. He didn't keep pulling the trigger. Like he knew he had exactly six chances to—"

"Bruce isn't my brother-in-law. He and Liz aren't married. And I know what I said, but my ears were ringing. It was loud and I was in shock—"

"Everybody was in shock. Everybody's ears were ringing. We retrieved slugs from, as you say, the floor, ceiling, door, wall. And one from your husband's body. Never did find the one that was fired out the window. So we have the bullets, but no casings, no weapon. Where did the gun go?"

VIVIEN, AFTER

"I have no idea. Maybe my sister hid it. Out of a misguided instinct to protect Clift."

"Maybe. Heat of the moment, irrational thinking."

"Exactly."

"So why would she not turn it over to us now? The heat of the moment is over. Three witnesses—you and both his parents—all claimed to have seen—"

"Bruce isn't—"

"Yes, yes, I know that. Do not be misled by the trivial. All three witnesses acknowledge Clift pulled the trigger. Saw the gun and saw Clift pull the trigger. Yes?"

"Yes."

"So that then is a fact. A fact. Not a theory, not a supposition. A fact. So, then, where did that gun go? There is, at this point in time, no reason for anybody to conceal the weapon."

"I don't know what to say."

"There were only three people in the room, besides Clift. Why would any one of you want to hide the revolver after the fact? It puts me in an Agatha Christie frame of mind."

"Agatha Christie?"

"The way she would have written it. Like *Murder on the Orient Express*. You know that one?"

"I saw that one."

"Then you know. It wasn't one single person who committed the murder. It was a whole group of people. They took turns. That was the big revelation. I am a detective. I must consider every possibility, however unlikely, so for all I know the three of you were in it together. Maybe you each had your own private reasons for wanting Pastor Williams dead, so you took turns. Two shots each. And then tossed the gun into Clift's lap."

"Well, for starters, I saw a crime scene technician swab Clift's hands and wrists. I imagine that was to test for powder residue."

"You are correct. Do you have to smoke? It is killing my sinuses, and the smell gets in my clothes."

"Sorry. Stress."

"Makes my cat sneeze when she smells me. Sneezing fits. Over and over."

"It's out."

"The smoke lingers."

"I'll turn on the ceiling fan."

"Deeper."

"What?"

"Deeper. The ceiling fan. That will just drive it deeper into my clothes. The smoke."

"Yes. Certainly. Of course. I'll open the window. There's a songbird."

"There's a what?"

"Outside. A songbird. On a tree. Near the water branch. There's a songbird who sings sometimes."

"Branch?"

"Creek. Branch means the same thing as creek."

"I understand English."

"I know that. I didn't mean anything by it. Branch is more of a southern idiom."

"You don't sound southern."

"Neither do you."

"Touché."

"I wasn't trying to score a point."

"*Brook*. The word is brook. Brook means a small stream."

"Certainly. Brook. I believe both words mean the same thing. Branch and brook."

"Yes, but you said *water branch*. A redundancy."

"I hardly see how it's a redundancy. A redundancy is the unnecessary use of more than one word or phrase meaning the same thing."

"But don't you see? Water and branch mean the same thing. It would be like saying *water river*. Or *water ocean*. Or *water creek* even. Do you understand what I am saying? You are using two words that mean the same thing. Water and branch. Same thing. What is a branch if it is not water?"

"How about wood? Couldn't a branch be made of wood?"

The detective reddened.

Vivien pressed on. Went in for the kill. She *did* want to score a point. Anything to distract her from the humming. "I was talking about a bird. A songbird who sings beautifully from a nearby tree. You very well could have thought I meant a limb if I had said *branch* by itself. I could have meant a songbird who sings from a tree limb. You see? If I had simply said *branch*, it would have been unclear whether I meant tree branch or water branch. So I said water branch. For clarity."

He looked away from her. "As you say."

Vivien lowered her eyes.

The detective raised his.

"However, you could have saved us both a lot of time and grief if you had simply used the word brook. No fuss, no muss. Problem solved. Clarity, right out of the gate. You said it yourself. We all seek clarity."

Vivien got up and opened the window. No songbird anywhere in sight. Walking back to the couch, she noted to herself that the detective did not like to be anything other than the smartest person in the room. She sat down and waited for him to proceed.

"Thanks. Civilized people don't smoke. You understand. I guess it's just part of the celebration of life. But as you say, we swabbed the boy's hands, so we know he fired the weapon. Or *a* weapon. And even if that was in question—which it is not—I spent two hours with your sister and brother-in-law. Yes, I know, he is not your brother-in-law. It amounts to the same thing. They are broken. Annihilated. Everybody is capable of murder. I know that. But not everybody can frame their disabled child for murder. Elizabeth Briggs and her partner Bruce are certainly not capable of that. I do not suspect either of them in any way either through negligence or purpose."

"Purpose. Purpose is important. Critical."

"As is clarity."

"Agreed."

"Your husband had a gun registered in his name."

"Really? William wasn't a hunter. Not much of a sportsman."

"It was a .38. A revolver. Handgun. Not made for hunting. They're made for killing people. You understand?"

"Why do you keep saying that? Asking if I understand. If I don't understand something, I'll let you know." Her head hadn't hummed like this in quite some time.

"Of course. Yes. It is merely a habit. A regrettable speech pattern. You under—oh, there I go again. I must make myself aware."

"Yes."

"I think it is because I care so deeply about clarity. The gun. The .38. It is not meant for sport. Like all handguns, it has only one purpose. To kill people."

"You mean self-defense."

"You say potato. It all amounts to the same thing."

"Like creek, branch, and brook."

The detective scoffed.

"Are you saying William gave Clift the gun?"

"It is certainly a possibility. Great way to commit suicide. Unique. That would make more sense than anything else."

"And he wanted me to have the insurance money. He wanted to provide for me. And he knew that if he committed suicide—"

"It would null the insurance. No payout."

"To think that he was at the point that he wanted to end his own life, and his last thoughts were that I should be taken care of. Wow. I'm getting emotional."

Vivien noted that the detective noted that the suspect didn't look emotional. She looked the opposite of emotional. Flat.

It could be that way sometimes. She could wear only so many masks at once.

"Was your husband upset about anything? Despondent?"

"Uhm, no, not really."

"You hesitated, why?"

"Ne reason. I mean, it's just that we never really know what goes on in someone else's mind. Not really. But there was nothing that I'm aware of that would have upset William. Made him despondent or sad. He prayed through his troubles."

VIVIEN, AFTER

"Children?"

"Do you see any children? Do you see any photographs of children?"

"By choice?"

"Are you investigating my husband's death or are you investigating my uterus?"

He frowned. "Marital discord?"

"No. Not really. Unless you count boredom as discord."

"I don't."

The detective made a show of sniffing his lapel.

He said, "Branch and limb do not mean precisely the same thing. They are different words with distinct meanings. A branch is smaller. An offshoot from a limb. Limbs are the larger."

"Fine."

He folded the lapel back into place, brushed it with his fingertips, and continued with his point of discussion—because *fine* was not a sufficient response. *Fine* was a dismissive response. "In any case, branch has several meanings. *Several*. Do you hear what I am saying? Several. Multiple. In the Bible for instance. You know the Bible?"

"I said I'm from the south."

"Then, yes, you know. In your Bible, the term *branch* carries both literal and symbolic meanings, often representing offspring, lineage, and even the Messiah, your Jesus. It signifies growth, new life, restoration, fruitfulness, and connection to a source of life."

"Fascinating. I would tell my husband, except his branch of the family is dead."

"You mock."

"I most certainly do not mock. You condescend."

"All I am saying is you should have said *brook*, not *water branch*. Brook would have conveyed your meaning. It would have been perfect. Brook would have been le mot juste."

"Well, the word *brook* itself has more than one meaning. If I'd said there was a songbird who sings in a tree by the brook, you might have accused me of saying it was a bird that sings by tolerating something. That I was saying that while the bird doesn't really *like* singing or *approve* of singing, it *brooks* singing. Because that is the other meaning of the word brook— allowing or tolerating something. As in, *neither I nor the songbird will brook any more of this discussion.*"

The detective again scoffed. Louder this time. Resurrected, he lunged. "That's a bit of a stretch. *By the brook* is a prepositional phrase. The object of a prepositional phrase is always a noun or pronoun. As the object of the prepositional phrase *by the brook*, there is only one possible interpretation, that the speaker is using the word *brook* in its noun form—a small stream."

She looked away from him. "Touché."

VIVIEN, AFTER

They both stared at the floor for a moment. A long moment—depending on one's perspective.

"We are being silly. How silly of us."

"Yes. You're right. Silly."

"Silly. Yes. And if you are more comfortable smoking a cigarette, you should smoke a cigarette."

"I wouldn't dream of it."

"No. No, I insist. It is your house, after all. Your house, your body, your choice."

"That's true. It is my choice. But my choice can affect other people. My choice affects you, because you will also breathe the smoke. We breathe the same air."

"Yes, yes, that is why I give you my permission. You understand what I am saying? That is why I insist. Your choice and my choice are aligned."

"Are you sure?"

"Yes, I am making an informed decision. I know full well the dangers of second-hand smoke. And yet, still, I insist you smoke."

She reached for the pack. "Well, if you insist."

"I do. I insist. I was behaving petulantly. Like a petulant child."

Vivien lit the cigarette. The suction from her lips drew the flame into the tobacco.

She was drawn to the light. The light was drawn to her. She merged with the light.

"You probably think I am the type of person who needs to always be right."

Pulling smoke into her lungs, Vivien shook her head to communicate that was not at all the case.

"That I need to be correct. The smartest person in the room."

Vivien blew a stream of blue-white smoke toward the open window. Where was that songbird?

"These perhaps are not desirable qualities for inter-personal relationships. It is probably why I am not married. No friends. But they are traits that make for a good detective."

Flicking carbon particulate into a glass ashtray, Vivien nodded. Her head was humming like a power transformer.

"But suicide still wouldn't explain what happened to the gun after the shooting."

Again, they both stared at the floor. Vivien refused to break the silence. She knew about tactics the police used to trick people into saying things they might regret later.

He prompted, "Why would anyone carry the gun away?"

"Isn't it possible one of the first responders took it, then lost it?"

"I considered that."

"That would make the most sense. I mean, they took Clift into custody. Took him out of his chair and threw him in the back of a squad car."

"Threw him?"

"Placed him. He can't support himself. He just flopped around and sank to the floorboard. Wedged there. Liz was screaming. Hysterical. One officer restrained Bruce."

"Yes. It was a bad night. Ugly. I've seen worse."

"I haven't."

"No, I guess not."

"In all that movement, all that turmoil, securing the body, removing Clift from his home, to the police car, to the emergency room, to the jail, to DFCS foster care, all that. Surely, it's possible the gun just got lost and nobody wants to take responsibility."

"Yes, it is a lengthy chain of custody. Plenty of chances to lose a piece of evidence. You're right. But the problem is there was never a gun to lose."

"Of course there was a gun."

"Of course. Yes. I'm not saying it was metaphysical. A product of the pain-body. Those bullet holes didn't manifest themselves."

"The pain-body. You read Eckhart Tolle?"

"A little. A little Tolle, a little Krishnamurti. *Upanishads*."

"Krishnamurti? Really?"

"Yes. His observations ring true. The chattering mind. We waste so much time, our minds ceaselessly chattering. You follow?"

"Yes, I follow. The internal monologue."

"At least a monologue has purpose. K was talking about mind chatter and how it serves no purpose. It never stops, and we try to suppress it, so there is—"

"Duality."

"Exactly. Struggle."

"Resistance."

"Conflict, yes. The point is, the responding officer, the first officer on the scene, stated in his report that there was no weapon on the premises. It could have been hidden. In a drawer. Under a couch cushion. In a tree by the brook. Anywhere. But it was not on the observable premises, and each witness remembered seeing the gun but denied knowledge of the weapon's whereabouts."

"People lie sometimes. To cover up for mistakes."

"Yes, they do. Resistance. When they would be better served to accept the current situation. Accept it. Take action if necessary. Move on if prudent. Either way, accept the present moment. But people do lie. Are you referring to the responding officer or the three witnesses?"

"The officer. He seemed nice. I'm just trying to think this through."

"Me too. You wouldn't happen to have your husband's gun, would you? Here in the house?"

"Not to my knowledge. I told you; I didn't even know William owned a gun."

"Would you mind looking for it?"

"No, I don't mind. But I wouldn't know where to start."

"Could you take a look now?"

"I wouldn't be comfortable with that."

"Why not?"

"As I told you, I don't know where William stored the gun or even if there *is* a gun. Just because you say William had a gun, that doesn't make it a true statement. Maybe he never owned a gun, and your computer got it wrong. William Williams. That a repetition of a very common name. Hardly a name at all."

The detective made a show of referencing his notes. "Yes, more like a title than a name. Registered to one W. Williams at this address."

"And it's possible William had misgivings about gun ownership and sold it."

"There would be a record."

"Or destroyed it. Threw it in a river. One less gun in the world."

"Please just look for it, ma'am. Can you promise me you will look for it?"

"Yes. But I feel I should talk to a lawyer. I don't want to somehow muddy William's reputation. His standing in the community." The humming in her head had was speeding up. The transformer threatened overload. Sometimes our circuits get shorted. By external interference. Signals get crossed.

"That's up to you. But if you have trouble finding it, we can get a search warrant and help you look."

"That's not going to be necessary. What if I found it, and it did turn out to be the gun Clift used, what would that mean?"

"What *would* that mean?"

"I don't know, that's why I'm asking you."

"You probably should get a lawyer. You understand what I am saying to you? but if it turns out that gun *is* in this house, and it's a ballistics match, one question that would need answering is how did the .38 get from the Briggs's house back to this house? There's really only one answer to that question."

"Yes?" The humming was exquisite. Building and building. Seeking the exact pitch, the precise frequency that would separate the hemispheres of her brain like continents drifting apart.

"There's only one way it got back here. You brought it back here."

"And why would I do that?"

"Again, I can think of only one answer. There is only one possibility. Your husband ended his own life. You have heard the expression of suicide by cop. This is more like suicide by Helen Keller. And you realized that. You knew he had been depressed. Upset over something. Even your sister and not-a-brother-in-law noted Pastor Williams had not seemed quite himself lately. Distracted. Out of tune. He *was* depressed, right?"

Vivien didn't take the bait.

"My theory is you recognized the shooting for what it was. And tried to cover up for your husband. That's why you would have taken the gun home that night."

"I think you might be getting a little Agatha Christie again. But it does make sense. William was a spiritual leader of this community. It would make sense that his wife would take action to preserve his legacy. To cover up an ugly suicide. It would let so many people down. Cause a crisis of faith. Ripples that go on forever. I can see why a good wife would want to cover that up."

"A good wife, yes. A good wife would stop those ripples before they start."

"I don't care about money. Do you believe that?"

The detective didn't take the bait.

"Come now. Answer. Shame the devil."

"What is this *shame the devil*?" Of course he knew what it meant.

"Telling the truth is seen as bringing clarity and exposing the darkness of lies, thus shaming the devil."

"Ah, yes. Yes. Another charming southern colloquialism?"

"How would I know?"

"Indeed. How *would* you know?"

"How about a charming Latin colloquialism? *Stet*. Let it stand. The question stands: I don't care about money. Do you believe that?"

The detective stood up to leave. He looked in her eyes. *Swirl*.

He shamed the devil and answered honestly. "Yes. Yes, I do believe that."

● ● ●

There was no insurance policy. She knew that. Single, double, or triple indemnity. It had been a bluff. A means to poke and prod at the truth.

He probably didn't even have a cat.

She liked him.

These Things Are Preprogrammed into Us

HE WAS IN A FOSTER HOME. RESPITE SERVICES, THEY CALLED IT. She believed DFCS ordered it. For Clift's safety. Vivien wasn't sure who orchestrated it. Some governmental agency. Clift wasn't allowed to be in his own home. Not until they figured out where he got the gun. They couldn't very well let him live in a house where someone gave the disabled young man access to a firearm.

Guns were the new smoking. The last time Vivien had gone to the doctor, they had asked a series of health screening questions. Do you use tobacco? Do you have more than two alcoholic drinks in a day? Do you eat fast food? Do you use illegal drugs? Do you misuse prescription drugs? Do you have a gun in your home?

No, no, no, no, no, and no.

But Clift had a gun in his house. That checkbox couldn't be unchecked.

The woman who opened the door (the foster parent?) was heavy. Her fat deposits formed rings. Rings of fatted skin around her wrists, around her neck. Outlines of fat rings could be distinguished under her gingham blouse. She smiled at Vivien, but it felt simulated—for show. A thought flashed through Vivien's mind that this woman sometimes abused the children and disabled adults who circulated through her home. Not sexually. Not even physically. But somehow, she abused them. Perhaps just by exposing them to her negative energy.

The woman shook Vivien's hand, then pantomimed a dramatic recoil. As though a physical force had repelled her.

"Sorry. I'm allergic to cigarette smoke. Very sensitive to the odor."

"Oh, I'm sorry," Vivien said and made a quizzical expression to indicate she had no idea where the odor was coming from, but it certainly wasn't emanating from her.

"You might have been around a smoker recently. The smell gets trapped in your clothes. In your hair."

"I don't think so, but maybe."

VIVIEN, AFTER

The woman fanned her hand, simultaneously waving away the odor and dismissing the idea Vivien might be responsible for it. "Clift's ready for you. Got him all cleaned up and dressed and in his chair."

"Okay, good. Is it okay for me to be alone with him?"

"Oh yes, absolutely. He has the right to visitors and to privacy. One hour max. I just need you to sign this visitation log."

She handed Vivien a clipboard with a ballpoint pen attached by a frayed length of twine.

"Here. Right here. And print your name, too. Legibly. And your address. Good. That's perfect. State rules. I have to be in compliance. I have to maintain my license. They do inspections every six months. Good. Okay. And I do need to check you ID."

Vivien retrieved her driver's license, and the woman took it. She grasped it greedily, and Vivien noted even the woman's fingers were rippled with excess fat. Coded into her DNA. These things are preprogrammed into us.

Without asking permission, the foster parent woman scanned the ID card with her phone, then tilted the phone up to point it at Vivien. There was a simulated shutter sound, and the woman had taken Vivien's photo before Vivien had the chance to decline or request explanation for the need of a photograph.

It didn't matter. The woman was already walking away, and Vivien followed her down the hallway.

Journey to Enlightenment

THE FOSTER WOMAN MOTIONED TO A DIGITAL CLOCK ON THE particleboard dresser. She frowned, then straightened the clock so that it squarely faced Vivien and Clift.

"One hour."

Vivien noted the time and nodded.

Then they were alone in Clift's room. She held his hand. They existed in stillness together.

Vivien became conscious of her breathing. The diaphragm expanding. The air moving in and moving out of her body. Breathing is the only body function that is both voluntary and involuntary. We can breathe consciously or unconsciously. Most of the time, we breath unconsciously. But right now, in the present moment, Vivien consciously breathed. To root herself in the Now, in the present moment. This was the first time she had practiced this meditation with another person. With another purpose.

She imagined a vast field of light. She and Clift, their manifested forms in the vast field of light, and as they breathed in through their noses, the light entered their bodies, and as they exhaled through their mouths, the light exited. The light was entering and leaving their physical forms in an endless cycle, until there was no difference between the light entering and the light leaving. It was a continuous cycle, until it wasn't a cycle at all. Vivien's physical form fell away as the light was within her and the light was outside of her. There was no inside. There was no outside. And there was no her at all. She was the light. And Clift was the light. The Source. All was One, and the dream of form, the dream of separateness, was exactly that—a dream.

She opened her eyes, and everything looked different now. The light was shining from everyday objects. From the table, from the floor, from the chair, from Clift's wheelchair.

From the gun in her hand. Light. The Source.

She wondered if Clift was on a journey to enlightenment. Did his mind chatter ceaselessly, or did he understand his mind was not his true Self? Perhaps without the stimuli of sight and sound and only limited interaction with the manifested world, Clift was more identified with the Source. With the unmanifested through which the Source of all life flowed.

She thought of the detective and his knowledge of thought and body as form. The thoughts of the physical mind as opposed to the observer who witnessed those thoughts.

She thought of duality. She had merged with the light, the Source. But now she had returned to a state of duality. Now she could be either inside her body or outside. She could be the observer or the observed. She could exist on one side of the coin or the other. The Source was both sides simultaneously.

How could she merge with the light? The Source. She had just entered the state of Being—pure Being—and returning to the physical realm was debilitating. She could feel her heart beating, her lungs breathing, her cells dividing. Her brain thinking.

How could she enter the state of Being and remain there? How could she exist permanently in the realm beyond form?

She took the chrome-plated .38 and placed it in Clift's hand. It was loaded.

Clift smiled. His body spasmed with joy.

If the gun discharged, the foster woman would come rushing in. Or perhaps cower in the hallway and call 911. Vivien doubted that she (Vivien) would be here, in this form, when the police arrived.

She thought about William. The idea that William had committed suicide by Helen Keller as the detective so snidely put it. She toyed with that concept. Suicide. Was it the coward's way out? Or was it the ultimate testament of faith? What form of enlightenment could exist on a higher plane than suicide?

But William wasn't seeking enlightenment. Not that she knew of. We have no way of knowing another human being's true feelings. Their true thoughts. We all emanate from the one source, but our physical forms are all different. The manifestation of the unmanifested. She had no idea what ceaseless chatter filled William's mind. What it told him. Would his mind have told him it was better to commit suicide than destroy the faith of others through divorce? It seemed silly. And without forethought.

Certainly, William believed suicides went to hell. And hell was a long time compared with the eye-blink that was a life of form.

Clift held the gun. His finger found its way over the trigger. The safety was off. He waved the gun wildly in his two-handed grip, pointing up, pointing down, pointing toward the window. And for a moment pointed it directly at Vivien. The weapon aimed at her heart.

If he had been pulling the trigger, emptying the chambers, Vivien surely would have died.

VIVIEN, AFTER

But Clift never pulled the trigger. Not once.
She rewarded him.

In the Midst of Heaven
(*Meet ME in the Middle of the Air*)

S HE LIKED TO SPEND TIME IN NATURE.

Cattail seeds floated—seemingly random—in the air, in the light.

God could be found anywhere. Jesus said, "Split a piece of wood: I am there. Lift a stone, and you will find me there." She didn't have to be in nature to feel God's presence, but it was easier. She saw God floating in the cattail fluff. Inconsequential, yet beautiful and sacred.

Jesus said, "I am the light that is over all things. I am all."

Vivien ran through the field, dancing in the white flurries.

I'll touch Jesus.

She jumped and tried to catch a spidery puff but couldn't get high enough.

I'll touch Jesus.

She tried again, but they were out of her reach. Calling on her higher-self to lift her, Vivien jumped again.

I'll touch Jesus.

Time slowed.

Suspended in the middle of the air, looking down, she thought, *feels pretty good up here.*

Vivien floated. She touched Jesus.

She grabbed the floating seed. It melted in her hand. It didn't melt like a snowflake, but like the melting clocks in the Salvadore Dali painting, *The Persistence of Memory*. The cattail fluff just went limp, flaccid. As though her touch had robbed it of vitality.

In the middle of the air, you can release yourself, but the only way to go is down.

Vivien's descending form—a bright, vessel blazing in the brilliant sunlight—looked like an iron nail. Threatening to pierce the earth. Threatening to cause a rift or schism. A tectonic shift.

Even now, falling, she was in the midst of heaven. Always had been, always would be. She wished she hadn't told William she didn't believe in God. Because she did. In fact, she believed in God more than William himself had. She saw that now.

   The eagle soars because the eagle soars.

   The eagle is God.

A Vector of Blame

"WHEN DID YOU START SMOKING?"

"Stress. I've been under a lot of stress."

"Smoking will just make it worse. Add to your problems."

They were on the back deck at Liz's house. The scene of the crime. Really, the living room was the scene of the crime. They tended to stick to the kitchen or the back deck.

"How is Bruce?"

"He's lost. I don't know if he'll ever get over this."

So many unanswered questions. The removal of their child from their home. Adult Protective Services. Department of Child and Family Services. Department of Behavioral Health and Developmental Disabilities. The police. The DA's Office. Entities and organizations and bureaucracies were lining up to get it on the action.

If only they knew how a revolver ended up in Clift's hand, that would provide an area of focus. A vector of blame. Of prosecution.

"What's the name of that perfume you're wearing? I really like it."

"Eternity."

"Of course. I might get some."

"You'll need it to cover up the smoke smell. It gets in your clothes. In your hair. Smoking is death."

Vivien reached into her purse and placed a pack of Salem 100s and William's .38 special on the patio table.

"I am become death."

Escape from Emptiness

THE MEETING WITH THE ASSISTANT DISTRICT ATTORNEY WENT well. The detective was there. Liz and Bruce and Vivien. They hadn't engaged a lawyer. Not yet. They wanted to retain the illusion of naiveté.

"We don't want to prosecute. Not anybody. We understand why Mrs. Williams took the gun. To protect her husband. His memory."

"Clift. Mainly I was protecting Clift. And William, too. I didn't know what had happened. I was scared."

The detective said, "Most human action is rooted in fear. Krishnamurti said fear is flight away from emptiness."

"This is suicide—"

"Exactly. What is suicide but escape from emptiness? Fear."

"I was scared for Clift, scared for William. Scared for Liz. I don't know why I did what I did."

"This is suicide," the ADA repeated, anxious to say his peace before anybody said anything incriminating—or philosophical. People's actions were often rooted in stupidity. "And we don't prosecute suicides. Assisted suicides, sometimes, but this was not assisted suicide. If William Williams had survived the…incident, he's the one we would prosecute. Reckless endangerment. No one here. No one in this room bears any responsibility."

"And Clift?"

"Clift least of all. He's the only true victim."

"He can come home?"

"Yes. Yes, of course."

"This is over? We can—we can relax now?"

Vivien had always been relaxed. She had accepted the life circumstance. The so-called problem. She had accepted it with serenity because she accepted the present moment.

"It's over. We'll have Clift transported home tonight."

Liz grew tearful. Wiped the emotion away with the back of her hand.

VIVIEN, AFTER

• • •

On the way out, Vivien and the detective were the last to pass through the door. He touched her elbow. As she turned around, he presented her with a card.

"My personal number. Call if you like. If you want company. Someone to talk to."

She accepted the card.

The detective shrugged, "We could talk about K. Or nothing at all."

Nothing At All

"THERE ARE OVER TWO TRILLION GALAXIES IN THE UNIVERSE, were you aware of that?"

Vivien took a sip of her coffee and said, "No. What does that even mean?"

The detective said, "That's just in the observable universe. The part we can see. Who knows, maybe the piece of the universe visible to us is, in actuality, less than a tenth of one percent of what exists."

Vivien didn't respond to this. No response seemed like the appropriate response.

"It speaks to our relative importance in the overall scheme. It speaks to scale. In practical terms, two trillion is two-thousand billion. Two-thousand-billion galaxies. And there are billions of stars within a single galaxy. Imagine it."

Vivien felt the coffee flow bitterly over her tongue. She suppressed an urge to flick her tongue over her lips. "That's not conceivable. I can't place any sort of perspective on that."

"It's impossible. Beyond the scope of the human mind to conceptualize. To fathom that grand of a scale. Two-trillion galaxies. Billions of stars within a single galaxy. And their solar systems. Our galaxy, the Milky Way, all by itself has four-hundred-billion stars. Four-hundred-billion stars in the Milky Way alone. And at least—*at least*—that many planets."

They sat in silence for a moment. Vivien was aware of the background chatter of other people, the sound of a cash register keys, the hum and gurgle of an espresso machine, street traffic outside. And the silence that allowed those sounds to exist.

"If you shrunk our entire solar system down to the size of a quarter, the sun would be microscopic. Not even a speck of dust. Do you follow? The planets would likewise be microscopic. If our solar system were the size of a quarter, then our Milky Way galaxy would be roughly the size of the United States. Imagine flipping a quarter out of an airplane. And it lands in Wyoming or something. Imagine if you had to find that quarter somewhere in the United States. That's what it would be like finding our solar system within the Milky Way. And the Milky Way is our neighborhood. It's our neck of the woods. Terra cognita."

He took a sip of coffee. "The universe is mostly empty space. Did you know that?"

"No." Of course she knew.

"I'm rambling. I find it fascinating."

"Do you want to come home with me? My house is mostly empty space."

Dear Vivien, Won't You Come Out to Play?

THEY HONEYMOONED IN INDIA.

It was a honeymoon-cum-spiritual pilgrimage. She kept the Williams surname. It was a little late to reinvent herself. On paper.

They saw the sights (the Taj Mahal, Fatehpur Sikri, Agra Fort, Akbar's tomb, Ram Bagh, and Sikandra Fort) and attended group mediation in a tent city. Indulged in the local cuisine and habits. Vivien was quite taken with smoking hookahs.

Of course, J. Krishnamurti was as dead as Alan Watts, but Eckhart Tolle was there on tour. And Sadhguru Jaggi Vasudev, a guru Vivien was less familiar with (she had his book but hadn't read it). She became quite taken with him. Sadhguru focused on the trinity of mind, body, and spirit. He had many famous followers. There were people in attendance that Vivien recognized from superhero movies and singers of pop songs that permeated American culture. It made her think of the Beatles visiting Maharishi Mahesh Yogi's ashram in Rishikesh in the 1960s. The actress Mia Farrow had been there too, with her sister, Prudence. The Beatles wrote a song about Prudence Farrow because she was so shy and reclusive. She wouldn't come out of her tent.

Vivien imagined the boy band that was in attendance for Sadhguru might write a song about her.

Dear Vivien, won't you stick out your tongue? La-di-dah, round, round, round...

She and the detective tried to figure out what spiritually enlightened love looked like. What did it feel like? Neither one of them was sure. Eckhart Tolle had some thoughts. Basically, most love isn't love at all. It is seeking meaning externally, through another, and therefore doomed to failure—as are all external things. But true love is recognition of the formless by the formless.

The formless, timeless intelligence.

VIVIEN, AFTER

Vivien forswore cigarettes and bought an expensive, ornate, marble-based hookah pipe. She knew it was purely symbolic, an unneeded external portal to travel within herself, and just as deadly as commercial cigarettes. But, again, the means of death are so sweet.

She put it on the living room table when they got back. The detective didn't object.

Bette Davis Eyes

THE DOORBELL RANG AT 12:34 A.M.
Vivien checked the camera feed and recognized the obese woman standing at her front door.

Vivien hissed into the microphone, "Yes, may I help you?" The detective snored beside her.

"We need to talk. Now."

There was something in the fat woman's voice, a commanding tone that bespoke consequences if denied.

Vivien did not have a guilty conscience. She didn't feel that she had been *caught*, (or potentially caught). The self with which she currently identified did not honor ego-bound emotions such as guilt, culpability, resentment, fear, sympathy, etc. Those were the baggage of the *me*. Such emotions were alien to her higher self. Only her egoic self was prone to base thoughts and feelings. And yet, inescapable, the witnessing-self observed that the egoic mind had an all-consuming thought. Like a flashing neon sign. *Danger.*

•••

Vivien unbolted the door and stood in such a way as to bar the woman's entrance into her home. The woman ducked under Vivien's outstretched arm and entered the foyer.

"This will be fast. But first, I just have to say, I knew from the second I laid eyes on you, something was off. It's your eyes. You have eyes like a sociopath. You have Ted Bundy eyes."

"I've been told I have Bette Davis eyes."

"Not quite, my dear. They look human, but really, they're more like…"

"A reptile?"

"Yes," the social worker gushed in an almost friendly tone. Like two women in a chiropractor's office who discover their backs ached in exactly the same spot. "Yes! You look like you belong in a glass aquarium, under a heat lamp. Perched on a stick."

VIVIEN, AFTER

Vivien licked her lips and reached behind the woman to pull the front door closed. She couldn't see any of her neighbors. Privacy hedges obscured the view.

"I've had sociopaths through my home. Teenage boys, mostly. Firestarters. Animal torturers. Sibling molesters. I recognize you."

"I don't understand. What do you want? It's..." Vivien glanced at the wall clock. "It's 12:34 in the morning." But it had been 12:34 five minutes ago. 1234five. The clock must be slow. She didn't want to glance at her phone to confirm this. She wanted to maintain focus, to stay present in the current moment and honor it with her deep attention. Nonetheless, both her enlightened-self and her egoic-self noted the synchronicity that was alive in the present moment.

"I couldn't get you out of my mind." The woman glanced at the marble-based hookah on the living room table. "Fancy. You're a fancy dope fiend. A hashish housewife. A regular Fu Manchu opium smoker." She looked at Vivien, an I-knew-it-all-along gleam dancing in her eyes. "I didn't like the fact that you closed the door when you visited with your nephew. I had a gut instinct you were abusing him somehow. Psychological. I don't know."

Vivien did not share that she'd had the exact same instinct about this woman.

"I kept thinking about you. And I read Clift's case file. How you people kept that out of the news is beyond me. It would have made fine reading. But I couldn't get you out of my mind. And I kept wondering, so I reviewed the security footage."

"Security footage?"

"Oh yes. It's standard."

Vivien remembered the woman adjusting the alarm clock on the dresser in Clift's room. "A nanny cam? Hidden in a clock? No, I don't think that is standard. Not at all."

The woman took a gulp of air.

"I've uploaded it. To a dark site. Illegal. The kind of site that can get the federal government watching you. The kind of site that sideloads viruses and trojans."

The woman held up an electronic device that was all but labeled with the word *burner*.

"Paid cash. It's not traceable to me. But I do have the original."

The woman awakened the screen and handed the glowing device to Vivien.

Vivien accepted it and glanced at the display. The name of the site was Paraphilia Dream.

The dream of form. The dream of broken *form.*

"You'll have to scroll down."

Vivien's thumb hovered over the smudged screen, realizing she was about to leave prints on the device. Incriminating prints, perhaps.

VIVIEN, AFTER

What did it matter? Vivien navigated deep into the page. Deeper, deeper, and deeper she scrolled past thumbnail images that promised obscenity beyond most human reckoning.

She scrolled past something familiar. Something that caused her heart to misfire. She scrolled back up. And, yes, it was a bit out of focus, but it was unmistakably her and Clift.

She couldn't stop herself. She played the video.

This Woman Is Very Much Dead

EVERYTHING WAS RIGHT THERE IN THE VIDEO. THE BEGINNING—the part where she held Clift's hand and they existed in stillness together—that part had been edited out. The video started with Vivien placing the gun in Clift's hand. Then, soon after, the act of physical union.

Vivien paused the video and handed the phone back to the woman.

"You're disgusting."

"No, *you're* disgusting."

"Please keep your voice down. My husband is asleep upstairs." And, to raise the stakes, she added, "He's a police detective."

"Then let's call him down," the woman said in a voice that was louder than before. "By all means, let's show him what you did to your nephew."

Vivien, struggling to stay in the present moment and accept it as it was, whispered, "What do you want?"

"I want to see you go to jail. I want to see your face on the news for what you did. But what I need is money."

"Money?" Vivien asked, as though she were not familiar with the concept.

"Yes." Quite loud now, almost shouting. "I'm blackmailing you. Extortion. I'll walk up those stairs right now and show your husband what he's really married to. He's married to a lower life form."

"I know what I'm married to," the detective said from the landing. He was wearing pajama bottoms and nothing else. "Let me see what you have on that phone."

"My pleasure." The woman smiled triumphantly and crossed to the detective, offering up the evidence. "That's online. There's nothing you can do about it. You can kill me, smash the phone, but it's a done deal. The Internet is forever."

The woman returned to the foyer, and while her back was turned, Vivien picked up the hookah pipe and in one smooth motion, swung the marble base down onto the back of the woman's head, smashing the brain stem—where God resided.

The detective looked at Vivien. They held each other's gaze for a long time, in stillness, then the detective stepped to the fallen woman and checked for pulse and respiration.

"That was a hard a blow. This woman is very much dead. You understand?"

Vivien understood the question was rhetorical.

The detective stood over the body and looked down at the phone in his hand. He began to scroll. Clicking on videos. He watched and scrolled for a long time. Vivien stood observing him and observing herself observing him.

"This site is highly illegal. It is probably monitored. Yes, highly illegal. But you, what you did with your nephew, that isn't illegal. It's immoral. Not biblically immoral. Lot had such relations with his daughters. Of course, Lot was drunk at the time."

Vivien just looked at him. There seemed to be nothing to say.

"He's an adult, not a minor. I suppose a case might be argued as to whether Clift was capable of giving consent. It certainly appears consensual. Do you understand what I am saying? A moment of bliss gifted to a young man denied most all the pleasures of the senses this physical world offers. Some might say you blessed him. Most would think it grossly inappropriate. None would deem it illegal. If the genders were reversed, and you were a lecherous uncle defiling a disabled niece, then perceptions might shift. Laws might be brought into play. But that is not the case. You killed this woman for nothing. Because she threatened to embarrass you."

He didn't see the part with the gun. Just the sex act.

"It's already passed. I can't take it back."

"No, you can't take it back."

"She bought that phone with cash. It's untraceable. She didn't access that site from her own devices."

The detective went to the kitchen. Vivien heard the utility drawer open. The detective came back into the living room holding a towel and a hammer.

"Start cleaning the blood. Use bleach." Through luck or serendipity or synchronicity, the woman had collapsed so that her head fell to rest on the tiled floor of the foyer. There was a lot of blood. But it would be easy to clean from the hard surface.

The detective wrapped the phone in the towel. Then he walked out the back door to smash it to bits with the hammer.

She Waits the Consummation

H E KNEW HOW TO DISPOSE OF A BODY AND A CAR. SHE HAD TO give him that. If you want to lose weight, ask an overweight person. They know all the secrets of weight loss. If you want to cover up a murder, ask a detective.

It involved fire.

Followed by water.

The ride home was noteworthy for its silence. He didn't ask her why. He didn't ask why, who, when, where, what. She had already communicated the basics.

The silence itself wasn't unusual. They tended to exist together in silence. They each respected the stillness from which awareness sprang.

They had not—thus far—consummated the marriage. Vivien did not dwell on this, but lack of physical intimacy was an itch in her ego-centric self. The self she no longer identified with.

They had talked about it in India. No, before India, when he first proposed a union. He said that all human relationships are born of ego, of the false self, and doomed to end in either failure or mutual resentment.

Love feels good, he had said. He felt love for her. He could be said to be *in love* with her, but ultimately, conflict would arise. It was inevitable. To say he was in love with her was a true statement, but love was only his egoic-self finding purpose through Vivien. It was good while it lasted, but it wouldn't last. It would end as all egoic relationships end. He furthered his point by saying that what the ego seeks is affirmation of its own reality.

"My lesser self, my unaware self, seeks happiness and contentment through you. I think, if I could have Vivien, *then* I would be happy. You see what that does? It makes you responsible for my happiness. Do you want that? Do you want to be responsible for someone else's happiness? It's too big a burden. A fool's errand. And of course, ultimately, there will come a day that you won't make me happy. And what will happen then? I will *resent* you. Why shouldn't I? You were responsible for my happiness. I pinned all my future desires on you. And you let me down. How could you not? The future doesn't exist. How could I make you responsible to provide me with something that doesn't exist?"

He went on.

"And perhaps you feel that you love me. What does that mean? It means you feel a deeper sense of aliveness when you think of me. When you think of me needing you, does that give your life more meaning? Does your life need more meaning? Does it need any meaning at all? Do I want the responsibility of giving your life meaning? Surely, I will fail."

There was a great deal more to it. Vivien couldn't follow it all, but she got the gist. And agreed with it. There was something about love and hate coexisting as two sides of the same coin and a special kind of love —true love—that exists beyond the self.

Then he said, "I feel joy when I am with you now. Joy comes from within. You can not affect my past or my future, because those things do not exist. All we have is right now. This present moment."

Marriage was a societal construct, and they lived within society, so why not?

Sexual intercourse, he said, was a manifestation of the physical self. Through the male-to-female union, there is bliss. Ephemeral bliss. It dissipates. As do our bodies, ultimately. The sex partner is an externalization of self. Just as the mind—its thoughts and emotions—is misidentified as self.

"But fear will always return when we seek self externally—through form, through the physical world. What could be more damaging than seeking self through another person? Through an object of love. Or an object of lust. You shut out everything else and focus on love or lust or both.

"You seek salvation, but salvation is in nothing external. So, where then is salvation? It is in the present moment that obliterates the future and the past. It is right here, right now. Your own Jesus told you as much. 'Even now, you are in the midst of Heaven.' How much clearer would you like it to be?"

• • •

When they got home, the detective gave her a blacklight for a final policing of the crime scene. Vivien found a spot of blood on the dining room wall. The murder happened at the front door, in the living room foyer area. She had no idea how blood could transport itself that far. It was a fine spray. A constellation of microdroplets.

She scrubbed it with water-diluted bleach. As she was returning the rag to the kitchen, the detective stopped her. He put his hand to her waist and physically stopped her. His hand ran over her body. Roughly. Rudely. Grasping, groping. He started to unbutton her blouse, grew impatient, and ripped the garment from her body. Pearl buttons lay scattered on the floor, like little opalescent planets.

The rending of the cloth had not been a smooth movement. It took a lot of force, and Vivien was jerked forward bodily. He ripped and ripped, tore at her undergarments, the great force causing abrasion, and her skin bled in spots.

They both saw the blood on her body, and she clawed at his face, tearing skin, drawing more blood. He knocked her to the floor, and she waited there for him, but he grabbed her by the hair and slung her across a dining room chair.

And thus they consummated their union through the ephemeral bliss of the manifestation of the physical self.

Reflections in a Golden Eye

Having thrown away the waterpipe—for obvious reasons—she craved nicotine. (The hookah was now at the bottom of George Sparks Reservoir in Sweetwater Creek State Park—near the ruins of a cotton mill burned down during the Civil War.)

Vivien sat with Clift in the Briggs's living room. Liz was in the kitchen. It had not been openly discussed, but Liz seldom left Vivien alone with Clift. Not anymore. Not for more than a few brief minutes. There were no more daytrips to the mountain. No more date nights for Liz and Bruce when Vivien stayed with Clift.

She didn't get it. It wasn't like the police report said Vivien had given Clift the gun. No, the report clearly indicated it was Vivien's suicidal husband who had done that. William put the weapon in Clift's hand. That was official. All Vivien had done was conceal the murder weapon after the fact. A grieving woman protecting her husband's legacy. Protecting the entire community from a crisis of faith. Her actions, according to the district attorney's office, were noble. Perhaps not well-considered, but noble.

Why was *she* being punished for William's sins? She had been found guilty by association. She was being punished, and Clift was being punished as well.

Liz poked her head out of the kitchen. To check on them. Perhaps to make sure Vivien wasn't unwittingly involving Clift in yet another murder.

When would the unwarranted suspicion end?

But Liz wasn't checking on Clift. She was checking on Vivien. She was making sure of Vivien's well-being. Her safety. Liz's gaze fell on her younger sister. A worry line creased her unblemished forehead. Her eyes held Vivien's eyes. Those Bette Davis Ted Bundy eyes. Communication rippled between the sisters.

Are you okay?

No, Vivien wasn't okay. Vivien had never been okay. Vivien likely never would be okay. Liz knew that. She knew her sister would never be okay. Not in this lifetime.

VIVIEN, AFTER

• • •

Vivien was aware Liz felt sorry for her. She knew that. Vivien had earned her sister's pity because of her barren state. Liz had been the one holding Vivien's adolescent hand during the procedure. Holding her hand as, legs splayed in stirrups, Vivien stared at the treatment room ceiling, the overhead fluorescent lights out of attunement and humming.

At the other end of pelvic exam table, she could feel the clinician inserting the instruments. Poking. Probing. Scraping. It hurt. It hurt *a lot*. She had been expecting lidocaine and nitrous oxide (per her research on the subject), but the clinic offered only ibuprofen. Liz objected, demanded narcotic pain management—anything less was primitive—but ultimately what they both wanted was for this event to exist only in the past, so she relented.

The doctor (a man) doled out the Advil and magnanimously advised a hot water bottle for any post-procedure cramping.

What should have taken a matter of minutes seemed to go on forever. Each second an eternity. Vivien had no idea that a single second could last so long. It was like each second gave birth to the second. It gave birth to itself, so that the second never ended. It was eternal.

She twisted away from the sharp, jabbing pain.

The doctor, irritated, said, "Stop moving. There'll be scarring."

"It hurts."

"I know. But you have to be still. You're a woman, not a girl. A woman bears pain."

The way he said the word *woman* sounded like a slur.

Vivien couldn't help it. She jerked away from the pain.

"Woman, you are going to cause me to perforate the uterine wall. Risking hemorrhage. We don't have the tools here to cauterize. If you hemorrhage, you shall surely die."

Vivien stopped moving. Liz squeezed her hand. There was a pause as the doctor selected a new tool. Vivien strained to peer over the Steri Drape and saw the instrument the man intended to use on her next. It looked like a knitting needle. No. No. It looked like a nail. Like a handwrought nail.

He went deeper. The lights hummed louder. The first second birthed the second.

Vivien then experienced what is often misidentified as an out-of-body experience, but really, it was more like a transparency overlay. A reality overlay. She became aware that she was outside of her body looking down on herself. Watching herself undergo the procedure. Her ethereal-self observed her corporeal-self having a paid-in-cash dilation and evacuation. Her first thought (from the air) was that there was far less blood than she expected.

VIVIEN, AFTER

Her lower-self looked up at her higher-self. Her higher-self smiled and said, "Feels pretty good up here."

Maybe, but it feels pretty bad down here.

"Meet me," the higher-self suggested.

Poke. Probe. Scrape. Deeper. Deeper. Each time deeper.

"Meet me. Up here. Won't you meet me?"

That sounded like a good idea. And as Vivien accepted the invitation, the pain grew remote, somehow theoretical, as though it were happening to somebody else, but she could still feel a blunted version of it. Like a conjoined twin, maybe.

poke, probe, scrape.

"Yes. Up here. Meet me in the middle of the air."

poke...probe...scrape...

"Feels pretty good up here."

The pain was gone. Most bodily sensation was gone. Pleasantly, Vivien could feel herself rising. Rising to meet herself in the middle of the air. She was right. Feels pretty good up here.

As she rose, Vivien looked back down and saw herself on the treatment table. Again, she was surprised by the paucity of blood, but even more surprised to realize she now existed in three states of being. She was herself on the gyno table, her rising self, and herself in the middle of the air. How many states were possible? How many transparency overlays could there be? Infinite? Infinite overlays of infinite Viviens. The idea overwhelmed her. Because she could see it. She could see it all. She could see everything. It was too much. The universe was right here in this room. The universe was part of her. She was the universe. There were stars everywhere. Black holes and dark matter. Spiral galaxies and supernovae. *The stars. My God, the stars*. It was too much. She was too young to experience this. She would rather be back on the table. But she *was* on the table. She could see herself right there on the table. In the middle of the stars.

All those stars, and it *still* feels pretty bad down there.

Already, another self was separating from the table-self, rising. Each self birthed itself. Her rising-self birthed another rising-self, and that rising-self birthed a rising-self. It was too much to comprehend. More than she wanted to comprehend. Because on top of all of that, on top of all those stars, it did feel pretty bad down there. Somebody was feeling it. Just not her. Who would save Table-Vivien?

She started to cry. All of her started to cry.

Her higher-self, crying, said "Relax. Don't worry."

Vivien was about to disagree, to protest that tears and worry were indeed called for in this situation, because she was replicating like amoebas on a newly-formed planet. But the higher-self shushed her and said, "Don't worry. Seriously. Do not worry. You are not here."

VIVIEN, AFTER

What did *that* mean? Of course she was here. She could see herself. She was *right here*. Where else could she be? Where else could any of us be? Here is what we know. Here is the one place we're always guaranteed to be. If you are not here, then where are you?

Surely to God she could do a better job of comforting herself than a trite paradox. A stupid Zen koan. *We know the sound of two hands clapping, but what is the sound of one hand clapping? If you are not here, then where are you?* There was no logical solution.

It was pablum. Odious, vomited pablum.

Then it hit her. There *was* a solution. Maybe not a cause-and-effect logical a solution, but the answer was right in front of her. The answer was self-evident. It was logical after the fact. You couldn't think your way to it, you had to see it all at once.

Viviens without number.

As she grasped the truth of those four words, *you are not here*, the fear evaporated. She was not here. What was there to fear? If you are not here, then nothing that *is* here can hurt you. Vivien rose from Vivien. Each Vivien birthed each Vivien. It felt more than pretty good. It felt amazing. The clarity of it. The *truth* of it.

The first truth born, another truth—an even greater truth—was about to emerge. It was crowning. The first truth birthed the second. She could feel it. The labor pains of its delivery.

She was on the cusp of making the most significant of discoveries.

The meaning, the purpose—*of everything*—was within her grasp.

A stainless-steel basin blazed—blinding. The reflective vessel caught the disattuned smear of the overhead light, distracting Vivien from the revelation that had almost been hers. The delivery of clarity, of ultimate truth, had been disrupted, aborted, and her higher-selves dropped back into her lower-selves—which was all just a matter of perspective anyway. The overlays folded back. The pages turned. The pain flared. The humming continued. It wouldn't stop. It was unbearable. The humming and the pain were equally unbearable. Each second gave birth to itself, so that the second never ended. The suffering went on forever.

Vivien closed her eyes and thought: *You are not here. You are not here. You are not here.* But she couldn't bring her higher-self back. Because, in fact, she *was* here. Trapped in the prison of immutable cause and effect. She had been so close to escape.

The poking, probing, scraping eventually ended. All things must pass. It was finally over. She had made it through. The procedure was now something that existed only in the past. She'd had to travel the length of the universe, through wormholes and defying the irresistible gravity of red dwarfs, worlds without number, but it was all behind her now. She could start the process of forgetting.

Liz was still holding her sister's hand when the disapproving doctor cleared his throat to get Vivien's attention. When Vivien opened her eyes, he showed her the clumps of unwanted tissue in the steel vessel and—eager to teach a young person a valuable lesson—condemned her, saying, "Woman, here is your son."

Liz was outraged, yelling at the doctor, her indignation electric, promising swift, career-altering repercussions, but Vivien couldn't be sure, because the humming had multiplied. Her head vibrated like a tuning fork.

She looked at what the doctor was holding. A loathsome jigsaw puzzle. The thing that had been in her womb (which wasn't human, not really) had been torn limb from limb. Dismembered and reassembled in the basin. To make sure the doctor had gotten all of it. Vivien gazed upon those pieces and considered what the future might hold for the contents of that bright basin. It's fate. She imagined Here Is Your Son would likely end up in an incinerator for medical waste, the carbon particulates vented high into the atmosphere, providing surfaces for water vapor to condense and then fall out of the sky in bright, blazing drops of rain. Or, perhaps, Here Is Your Son would be bagged and wrapped in red biohazard tape, a discreet packet destined for a landfill.

Dumped into a hole in the earth or set ablaze and emitted into the sky.

In those streaks and clumps of glistening tissue, Vivien could see white bone, sinew, and limbs like discarded doll parts. The bones—tiny, fragile bones, like a rodent—were visible where they had been stripped clean of flesh by the serrated metal teeth of a primitive tool. But worse than the bones, worse than the disjointed doll limbs, far worse than any of it, was the head. The skull had been crushed like a soft-boiled egg. She could see an eye. A delicate blue-gold iris. A *human* eye. How could something that wasn't human have a human eye? How was that possible? The eye seemed huge. The only thing Vivien could see was that eye. Communication rippled between them. Between her and it. Between her and the great, sightless, unblinking eye.

Remember me, Here Is Your Son insisted. *Remember me when you come into your kingdom. Your kingdom of water and ice.*

Her head was humming, and she couldn't get it to stop. That eye. That golden eye. It was dark, long-frozen blue-gold ice. Like looking into an arctic abyss. It was causing a glacial fissure in her head. A crevasse. A chasm. A calving. A great seizure that wrenched open her brain. A hypothermic schism of water and ice.

Hemispheres separated. Pangea split. Glaciers surged. Oceans disgorged upon the land.

VIVIEN, AFTER

Please, God, let it stop. Let the humming stop.
It didn't stop. It never stopped.
The humming overtook her.
Then darkness came.

• • •

Sitting on the Briggs's living room couch, so absorbed was she in thoughts of the past and thoughts of the future and the unfairness of her current circumstance, that Vivien was surprised to find her sister kneeling before her—between her and Clift in his chair—gazing up at Vivien. Liz reached out and rubbed Vivien's cheek with her thumb, wiping away a teardrop. Her thumb left a swath of stark coldness as the residual wetness evaporated. Water and ice.

"Viv, you have to move on. Do you understand?"
Vivien nodded, uncertain. "It hurts."
"I Know. But you have to forgive yourself. It's time. It's been long enough. Let it go. You must forgive yourself. You're the only one who can."
Vivien had no idea what her sister was referring to.
"I do. I do, Liz. Honestly, I do. I forgive myself."

• • •

Vivien considered the injustice of it all. In this, the present moment, she reflected on these considerable misfortunes that had befallen her. She considered the facts of the current situation. William's death. Is that what her sister was referring to? Was Liz suspicious? A careful observer might ask how did Vivien know it was William's gun? In that moment—the aftermath of the shooting—how did Vivien *know* it was her husband's gun? Didn't all .38s look pretty much the same? Vivien didn't know, but surely it must seem odd that she would look at the spent gun in her nephew's lap and recognize it as William's. And even if she had, even if she'd had the wherewithal to recognize the provenance of the revolver, why would she take it away from the murder scene? She couldn't have known it was a form of suicide—not in that moment. No one ever asked. Perhaps the answer was assumed to be that, on some level, she'd recognized William's dissonance, his despondency, his *disattunement*, and simply knew in her gut that he'd somehow been involved in his own death. So she covered it up.

But only *she* had the knowledge that the prospect of divorce might well have caused such dissonance—gotten her husband so out of harmony with existence. Out of attunement.

A quick cover-up out of misguided loyalty was the only rational explanation.

VIVIEN, AFTER

What no one ever considered was that Vivien might have trained Clift how to kill. That she purchased blank rounds. That she aroused and satisfied Clift with physical pleasure. That being deaf and blind left him a slave to tactile sensations. That Vivien carried a sealed plastic bag that held a handkerchief scented with William's cologne. That she taught Clift to fire the gun until it was empty (he learned quickly that six shots were all you get).

That she conditioned him so that after receiving the olfactory stimuli, he was to empty the gun, then be rewarded with physical pleasure.

It was operant conditioning. Straight out of B.F. Skinner.

Scent.

Fire.

Reward.

Operant conditioning. The consequence (in this case, a positive consequence—physical pleasure) is received after performing the specific behavior (firing a gun toward a specific scent).

When training him, she moved around, opening the scented bag from different orientations, so Clift learned to fire the weapon at the source of the scent. Sometimes with blanks, sometimes dry firing. The CP made it difficult, but with six shots, he could usually swing the gun in the direction of the target.

On the night of the incident, as they prepared to enter Liz and Bruce's home, she had sent William back to the car to fetch her phone. So that when he walked into the house, he entered alone. Reeking of that obnoxious Aqua Velva.

She'd had just enough time to corral Liz and Bruce into the kitchen.

No one ever thought how it came to be that the three of them were not downrange when the gunfire began. Not even the detective questioned this. At least not aloud.

Why, then, had Vivien concealed the gun after the fact? Why not leave it in Clift's lap? Hmmm… She smiled. Why indeed? Was it a spur-of-the-moment impulse born of fear, or was it premediated to make it more fun? To make the game more challenging? To prove she truly was a dark player. A cunning opponent.

The sex video was a bit of a wrinkle, but the detective had helped her iron that out. Destroyed the physical evidence. Destroyed the body of the blackmailing interloper. And through some bit of anonymous whistleblower reportage, had that website taken down. "The woman probably has a hard drive somewhere with thousands upon thousands of hours of secret video monitoring. Almost certainly encrypted. Even if it's not, the working assumption is she walked away. Abandoned her duties. State workers are not known for their stability. Her belongings will be put in storage and ultimately discarded. It's a loose thread that isn't a loose thread at all. Because, as I said, what you did wasn't illegal. Just the part where you killed her."

He was an odd sort, the detective. A real rara avis.

She wondered how much he knew. What he suspected. What he intuited. He was in tune with the universe. Spiritually in accord. Possibly enlightened. He certainly believed he was enlightened. So many people did. They posed as enlightened. But the detective didn't just talk the talk.

She wondered how deeply he had dug in his investigations. Did he know, she wondered, that Liz was rich? Did he know that Clift had been deprived of oxygen at birth? Lodged in the birth canal, the constricted umbilicus robbing him of life force. That the obstetrician had opted for forceps when a Cesarian would have been faster and prevented brain injury.

Liz hadn't pursued the promised legal action against the callous abortionist, but the Briggs had sued the delivery room doctor and the hospital for gross negligence. And they had not only prevailed but were awarded the largest malpractice settlement in state history.

Liz's husband, Clift's father, had decamped. Even with money, he couldn't cope with being the parent of a child so fundamentally disabled. He had a choice: to accept his life circumstance as it was, or to take action and change it. He chose change and walked away from the money and his family. He disappeared, never to be heard from again. And what did it matter? Clift couldn't hear anyway.

Liz met Bruce, and they were mostly happy together. They could live like royalty, but Liz said she wouldn't feel right living a life of luxury knowing it had been purchased at the cost of her son's good health.

The money was in Clift's name, but Liz, of course, was the legal guardian.

She controlled the money.

People who have children with significant disabilities worry about the future. They worry about what will happen to their child when the parent dies. Who will care for their child. And Liz, being a single mother, worried even more. Bruce was fine, she was glad to have him. Liz knew Bruce loved Clift like he was his own blood. But that was the point. Bruce wasn't blood. He was a live-in boyfriend.

Vivien was blood. Liz legally appointed Vivien and William Williams as Clift's guardians in the unfortunate event of her death.

Of course, William was gone now. So, it would be Vivien alone to administer the largest malpractice settlement in state history.

That is, if anything were to ever happen to Liz.

VIVIEN, AFTER

Making sure that they were unobserved, Vivien opened a Ziplock bag and let Clift sniff the sweetly perfumed handkerchief inside.

She placed her other hand in his lap.

The Suffering Goes on Forever

THERE SEEMS TO BE A MISUNDERSTANDING SURROUNDING THE word *sin*. Remember, sometimes words have two meanings. Most people consider sin a misdeed of some sort. An ethical or moral transgression. Adultery, murder, theft, fornication, etc. Or simply the desire to commit such acts. What is worse, committing a sin or the willingness to do so? According to Jesus, they are the same. What holds you back from committing that sin you long to indulge in? The threat of eternal damnation? Commit the sin or don't commit the sin. Either way, confess it to your priest and be forgiven.

Or don't confess it to anyone. Simply accept Christ into your heart and be forgiven. No matter what wickedness you might have indulged in, you are cleansed by the blood of the lamb. It's the ultimate get-out-of-jail-free card. The only catch is that you must actually believe and repent. You may then enter the gates of heaven and walk the streets of gold arm-in-arm with Jeffery Dahmer—who accepted Christ before his death at the hands of a fellow inmate.

The idea of the seven deadly sins also gives credence to this idea of sin being a specific act or a specific state of mind. Pride, greed, wrath, envy, lust, gluttony, and sloth.

The threat of hell keeps us not only from indulging in wicked acts, but keeps us from desiring to commit those acts, to think those thoughts, to feel those feelings. As with sin, there seems to be some misunderstanding as to the meaning or the concept of hell. Something was lost in the translation. Vivien certainly didn't consider herself a biblical scholar, but she knew enough to know that the Greek word *Gehenna* translates as both hell and Hades (the place of the dead). This word Gehenna is used twelve times in the New Testament. Jesus mentions Gehenna eleven times.

Hades is a place of torture for the sinners after death. Heavenly punishment. A celestial time-out.

Hades is temporary and only your soul goes to Hades. In Gehenna, however, the iniquitous dead exist in both body and soul. Gehenna is eternal. The suffering goes on forever.

Gehenna is the ultimate punishment. Not because of the torment, but because the physical body and the eternal self are forever entwined. You never awaken from the dream of form. The point of enlightenment is to transcend the mind and physical body, to become one with the Source.

Hell is the curse of eternal duality.

The dream of physical form never ends.

There is only one sin. And that sin is knowledge. Logic. Sophistry.

The reclusive writer, J.D. Salinger, so enamored of the Indian thinkers (and age-inappropriate relationships), said logic is what was in the apple Eve fed Adam.

They ate from the tree of knowledge. They lost sight of their oneness with God and entered the state of duality. And that's all any of us have been trying to do ever since—move past duality and see ourselves as divine. As one with God. One with the universe.

Duality is just another way of saying separateness. We experience ourselves as separate not only from God but separate from each other when we are in fact One.

But what has any of this to do with the reptile brain? Vivien's thinking had evolved, and she had come to believe that if we do indeed carry the light of God, then the reptile brain is the resting spot of that God-spark, that seed of divinity. And as we physically evolved, we lost touch with our God essence. It was buried in that part of the brain we no longer access. We evolved to the mammal brain with its limbic system and hippocampus. We kept on evolving into the neocortex—the hemispheres of language, abstraction, logic, art, and imagination. We live in a human brain tainted by logic.

Addicted to logic. We can't stop thinking. Chatter. Ceaseless, useless, repetitive chatter.

Under all these layers of mammal and human brain, our reptile brain lies unused, glowing with the forgotten light of God.

In fact, we actively suppress the reptile brain. It's the depository of primitive survival instincts. It's the oldest part of the brain, and therefore the closest to God. It holds the God-spark, yet we ignore it, push it to the side. Disdain it.

We disdain God.

• • •

Vivien researched the matter. What she found, what ultimately convinced her that her theory was correct, was this: The worst natural disaster (AKA an act of God) of the last century was the Indian Ocean Tsunami. The loss of human life was staggering. The tsunami originated with the most powerful earthquake ever recorded in Asia, causing the ocean to disgorge upon the land.

227,898 people were killed, their lives doused.

The human suffering went on for months, years.

It was, quite simply, horrific. It caused one to ask *why*. Why does God care so little for us that he would allow such a thing to happen?

But, Vivien wondered, what if we turned that question around and put the onus not on God, but on ourselves. What if the question such a tragedy provoked was not why would God allow this to happen, but why did we not listen to God?

Perhaps God told us, and we didn't hear. We didn't listen. Perhaps he showed us, and we refused to see. Because we are deafblind. Perhaps we've been so busy denying the reptilian brain, that we've shut ourselves off from God, from the universe. The Source.

The animals listened. The animals saw.

A wildlife reserve along Patanangala beach in Sri Lanka was devastated as the ocean swelled and massive waves engulfed it—killing all the human visitors. Yet no animal carcasses were ever discovered. Elephants were observed to scream and run away from the beach an hour before the tsunami arrived.

In many of the hardest hit areas, where human fatalities numbered in the tens of thousands—cats, dogs, and goats were found alive and well.

227,898 human beings were killed, but virtually no animals died in the tsunami.

How was that possible?

Our chattering minds (dominated by logic) want to find cause-and-effect. There must be a logical explanation as to why hundreds of thousands of humans perished, yet almost no animals died. We think to ourselves, the animals must have sensed some ineffable seismic shift. Some miniscule precursor that warned them to seek high ground. A blip in the magnetic fields. A scent in the air that is beyond our olfactory perception.

Maybe a few animals of each species sensed the looming disaster and alerted their animal kin. The way a field of grounded gamebirds might take flight simultaneously. Or how ants communicate with chemical trails.

No, we don't know what the reason is, but we are certain that by-God there *is* a scientific reason.

They *knew*. The animals knew.

Then why didn't we, the dominant species on this planet, get the celestial memo? Why didn't we get the fax from God? Why were we caught unaware and drowned en masse like kittens in a burlap sack?

VIVIEN, AFTER

Maybe we did get the memo. Maybe we did get the fax. But it went to our reptile brain. And we ignored it.

It's not necessarily insider trading. The animals may not have gotten a tip-off. They may have simply found themselves on higher ground that day. The same way Cormac McCarthy found a free tube of toothpaste in his mailbox when, penniless, he'd run out. The same way the lucky commuter decided to take the long way home the day a multiple-fatality pileup happened along their usual route.

It was what Carl Jung called meaningful coincidence.

It was synchronicity.

A Sober Person

SLOWLY BUT SURELY, TRUST WAS REESTABLISHED.
Vivien was allowed to spend time alone with Clift.

At first it was small matters of necessity. Errands that needed to be run, and Vivien was a convenient caretaker. Then she was allowed to walk with him around the neighborhood, even take him on nature hikes.

The presence of the detective in her life helped tremendously. He was an authority figure. A symbol of protection, safety, and stability.

There came a time when Liz and Bruce wanted to get away for a few days. To take a trip. A vacation, but not a family vacation.

Vivien said she would be happy to have Clift stay with her and the detective.

The detective did not object. He liked Clift. He said Clift was in harmony with his true self, his God-essence. That his oneness with the universe was on par with the most enlightened of thinkers. Clift's mind had not been polluted by the external world. Clift, he said, may very well be free of the delusion of physical form, and therefore not externally identified. Clift did not require a witness to his own thoughts to identify those thoughts as different from himself. He was free from the curse of duality. No ceaseless internal chatter to suppress, and therefore no struggle, no resistance to what is. Clift did not think of himself as two entities, as most of us do. Because he wasn't. And therefore, he would not be subject to the ultimate punishment—Gehenna. Hell. Where the physical body and the eternal self are forever entwined. Where you never awaken from the dream of physical form. Clift was already free of that dream. He was already enlightened. He had transcended the mind and the physical body. He was one with the Source.

Or he had been before the pollution of Vivien.

The detective believed the present moment is all Clift knows. He accepts each moment as it is. He does not resist what is.

VIVIEN, AFTER

When Krishnamurti was asked what his secret to enlightenment was, he said, "This is my secret. I don't mind what happens." The detective smiled serenely and explained the statement was deceptively simple. It meant that internally K is in alignment with the now. He does not resist the present moment. He does not label the present moment as good or bad but accepts it as it is.

The detective believed Clift had achieved (or had always had) a spiritual essence on level with Krishnamurti.

In fact, the detective suspected Clift was the reincarnation of J. Krishnamurti.

K reborn, he had called him. And perhaps this was his final life, his last incarnation in the karmic the cycle of birth, death, and rebirth.

The detective read to Vivien from The Bhagavad Gita: "Worn-out garments are shed by the body; Worn-out bodies are shed by the dweller within the body. New bodies are donned by the dweller, like garments."

The detective glanced up from the book, to see if Vivien was following. She was.

He read on: "Never was there a time when I did not exist, nor you, nor all these kings; nor in the future shall any of us cease to be. As the embodied soul continuously passes, in this body, from childhood to youth to old age, the soul similarly passes into another body at death. A sober person is not bewildered by such a change."

Perhaps, he had said, K had been born and reborn thousands of times. As a stone, a tree, an owl, a beggar, a king. As Jiddu Krishnamurti. And now as Clift Briggs.

The detective believed (or at least suspected) that K had chosen the physical form of Clift so that he might at last fully realize his divine nature and end the cycle of reincarnation. That through this present dream of form, spiritual liberation would be achieved.

"Of course, Krishnamurti himself did not believe in reincarnation. He didn't believe in anything."

Nonetheless, the detective enjoyed a chance to sit alone with Clift to bask in the stillness. He did everything but pray to the physically damaged deity. So, he was most accepting of the idea that Clift might spend a few days in their home while his mother and her boyfriend gambled at a Native American tribal casino.

• • •

Vivien took a rideshare to Liz's. To pick up Clift and get the lift van. She brought Liz a present.

It was in a small, plain craft bag with two loops of scratchy twine for a handle.

"It's from the detective."

"Oh, how sweet. Why don't you ever call him by his name?"

"That *is* his name. That's how he exists in my mind. As *The Detective*. The present is from him. You know how he is. Spiritual."

"He is that. You're both a little otherworldly."

"He got this from a Buddhist monastery. The monks make it by hand. It's soap and body oil. Specially scented."

Liz frowned. "You know I hate that hippie smell. What's it called… patchouli."

"It's not patchouli. It smells like heaven."

Liz brought the bag under her nose and sniffed. "I don't smell anything. She pulled out a cake of soap and sniffed. "This is hermetically sealed. Can't tell if I'm going to like it." She tried to find a seam in the multi-layered plastic to pry in a fingernail.

"No, don't open it now. It's sealed that way so the scent can't escape. The Buddhist monks believe the scent carries spiritual energy. Karma, or something. They seal it so none of the spiritual energy gets out. It's supposed to bring you luck."

Liz dropped the soap bar back into the bag. "I can use all the luck I can get. I'll try the body oil first."

Synchronicity

"VIVIEN, HAVE YOU SEEN MY SERVICE REVOLVER?"

"No. Where did you have it last?"

He looked at her, deadpan, and hit the side of his head with the heel of his hand—as though to dislodge water from his ear. "What?"

His skin glistened, fresh from the shower, a towel wrapped around his middle. The detective still had a good body. She admired that about him.

"Where did you have it last?"

"The bureau. On the bureau. Where it always is. When I got out of the shower, it wasn't there. You follow?"

The detective often peppered his discourse with little asides. Little questions that didn't necessarily deserve a question mark. *You understand? You follow? Do you hear what I am saying? You follow what I am saying? This makes sense?* Etc. These were not sarcastic or confrontational. They were the flavors of his speech. Although he spoke perfect English, these idiomatic implorations betrayed that English was his second language. He wanted to be sure he was expressing himself clearly. Sometimes they had the uplift of a gentle question, and sometimes the flatness of a benign statement. *You understand?* and *You understand.* Same thing.

She asked, "Are you sure you didn't leave it in your locker at the office?"

"I never leave it at work. You understand what I am saying?"

"You never leave it at work?

Pulling up his pants, he said, "That is what I just now said."

"You said 'at work?'"

"Yes. Why are you belaboring this?"

"Maybe it's on a tree. Hung on a tree. By the brook."

He finished buttoning his shirt before saying, "Is that funny?"

"No, it's not funny. I simply noticed that you said you never leave it at work. *Work* is the object of the preposition *at*. *Work* is a verb."

"*Work* is also a noun. Don't be funny."

"Yes, but you could have meant you never leave it at work, performing its function. The work—the labor, if you will—of a gun, is, as you once put it, killing people. Saying you never leave your gun at work could mean you never leave it shooting people."

"I believe my language was quite clear. I used *work* as a noun, not a verb. Nice try."

"My point is the object of a preposition is not always a noun or pronoun; it can also be a gerund, a noun clause, or a noun phrase."

"A gerund is a verb ending in *i-n-g* that functions as a noun—serving as a subject, direct object, or object of a preposition."

"Are you sure?" *Make him prove that he's the smartest person in the room. A title must be earned.*

"Yes, I am quite certain on this point. A verb cannot be the direct object of a preposition; the object of a preposition is always a noun, pronoun, or a clause functioning as a noun. However, to your point, a verb in its gerund or infinitive form can be the object of a preposition. For example, in the sentence 'I am thinking about going to the movies,' *going* is a gerund, a verb form ending in *i-n-g*, that functions as the noun object of the preposition *about*."

"What about the infinitive form of a verb? Couldn't the infinitive form of a verb be the object of a preposition?" *Make them question their own sense of reality. Are you sure? Are you sure you're sure?*

"The infinitive form of a verb is its basic, unconjugated form, typically appearing as *to* plus the verb. For example, 'to run,' or 'to eat.' This infinitive can function as a noun, adjective, or adverb in a sentence, expressing an action or idea rather than a specific, tense-bound action performed by a subject."

"You said, 'typically appearing as *to* plus the verb.' So not always. Give me an example." Being married to a detective, she had learned about tactics the police used to trick people into saying things they might regret later. *Give me an example* was one such example of the verbal manipulations employed by law enforcement. *Are you sure?* being another.

"As you say, in English, the infinitive is usually preceded by the word *to* forming a to-infinitive."

"Yes, we've established that. I want to know the exceptions to the rule." *Always push your point. Don't allow yourself to be diverted.*

"Infinitives do not have a tense or subject, and they are not conjugated like other verbs."

"Again, we have established that. I want the exceptions." *Do not relent.*

"Bare infinitives. Bare infinitives are the exception. English uses bare infinitives, which are the base form of the verb without *to.*"

"Can the object of a preposition be a bare infinitive?" *Stay on the offensive. You control the interview. Allow the other participant to have the illusion that it is a conversational exchange. Only you know the true goal.*

"No, a bare infinitive cannot typically be the object of a preposition in modern English grammar. Prepositions are usually followed by a gerund, not an infinitive form. However, there are rare, archaic constructions, typically biblical, where a preposition is followed by a verb form that resembles a bare infinitive."

"Please stop using the word 'typically'. Is the verb *brook*—as in suffer, bear, or endure—a bare infinitive?" *Press them. Don't relent.*

There was a twinkle in the detective's eye, a suggestion of a smile at the corners of his mouth, because he thought he now understood what she was up to. Settling an old score. "No, the verb *brook* is not a bare infinitive, but its base form, *brook*, can function as one. The term bare infinitive refers to a specific function of the base form of a verb, not the verb itself."

"Okay, fine. What is the base form of the verb *brook*?" *Let them think they have the upper hand. Mislead them into thinking they know your true intentions.*

"The base form of the verb *brook* is *brook*. That is the infinitive form of the verb, which is also the form used for the simple present tense, such as 'I brook,' 'you brook,' 'we brook,' and 'they brook.' Using your meaning, 'I suffer,' 'you suffer,' 'we suffer,' 'they suffer.' Are you concerned for your birdie on the tree by the brook? Are you afraid it may be suffering, bearing a burden, or enduring a tribulation?"

"Stay focused. What you said doesn't make sense. On the one hand you're saying the verb *brook* is not a bare infinitive, but its base form, *brook*, can function as one?" *Don't be misled by the trivial. Call them on their obvious lies. The inconsistencies in their story.*

"Yes."

"And the base form of *brook* is *brook*?"

"Yes."

"So, you are saying the verb *brook* is not a bare infinitive, but the exact same verb—again, *brook*—can 'function' as a bare infinitive? That's nonsense. Are you saying *brook* is a quantum word?"

"Yes."

A string of single-word answers always meant they had wised up.

"You're telling me *brook* can exist in multiple states at once, a sort of grammatical quantum superposition?"

"Yes."

"But how does that make—"

"Where is my gun?"

He'd seen through her. Never let them know that you know that they know.

"It's probably in your locker. At work. Hard at work."

"I never leave it at work. You understand what I am saying?"

"You did one time. I remember."

"I don't remember that. I think you may be mistaken."

"No. I remember it distinctly. You were distressed. Looking for it. You said you never leave it at work, so it couldn't be there. But it was. It was in your locker at work."

"Why do I not remember that?"

"I don't know. You can't even remember basic grammar, how are you going to keep track of your office equipment?"

He scoffed.

"The human mind is a funny thing. It tricks us. It tells us lies sometimes."

"Often."

"What?"

"The mind. It often tells us lies. The brain is a great trickster. A master illusionist. You understand."

"Well, I think your brain might be tricking you now. In this present moment."

"Perhaps. But my badge is here. The gun and the badge are always together. You hear what I am saying. Of that much I am certain."

"I'll help you find it. Finish getting dressed. Your socks don't match. Liz messaged me while you were in the shower. They should be here any minute to get Clift. Bruce will drive the van home."

∙ ∙ ∙

Downstairs, still searching, the detective glanced at Clift. He walked over to the young man whom he believed might very well be the reincarnation of Jiddu Krishnamurti and stroked his arm. Clift's body contracted and spasmed in response. It looked like pure joy. The difference between happiness and joy was that happiness depended on external conditions, while peace and joy came from within.

"Perhaps we have a few moments to sit in stillness with Clift. To be present in this moment together?"

As the detective's external focus switched from the whereabouts of his gun to the enticement of a few moments of communing with the soul of J. Krishnamurti, Vivien felt the universe align. She practically heard a click—as though another pin in the cosmic tumbler lock fell into place, opening the universe to her desires.

Synchronicity.

She joined Clift and the detective and opened herself to the present moment. To be deeply in the now. A state that most must consciously seek in order to attain consciousness from our habitual state of unconsciousness.

For Vivien, the path was through the inner body. She entered the state of being by (paradoxically) becoming aware of her physical form. The first step was conscious breathing. This quieted the background chatter. The background emotions. The Buddhist monk Thích Nhất Hạnh said, "Feelings come and go like clouds in a windy sky. Conscious breathing is my anchor."

Vivien used conscious breathing to anchor herself in the present moment, in the now. Thus moored, thoughts of the past and the future slipped away. She guided her thoughts to her inner body. Her physical form was but a dream, a shell of impermanence, yet it held the miracle of life. Eyes closed, she directed her thoughts to her feet, and felt the life energy within her toes. She shifted focus ever so slightly, to feel that life energy in her shins, in her thighs, her torso, arms, hands—until she felt her whole body infused with life. An energy that was within her and outside of her at the same time. She resisted the urge to think about this sensation, to intellectualize it. To apply logic. She merely witnessed. And saw that while her body stopped at the skin, her life energy, her God-essence existed inside and outside. The perception of separateness faded. There was no such thing as inside and outside. They were one. The energy that animated the body was the same energy that caused nuclear fusion at the core of the sun. She was one with the ever-expanding universe. God was within her, and God was outside her. But there was no inside and no outside. For a moment, she felt herself intellectualizing, identifying with her mind, trying to label the experience instead of just feeling it.

As she shifted back into alignment, there was a sensation of time once again slipping away. Memory and anticipation faded, so that she was no longer trapped in time, but back in the present moment—where all was well, she lacked nothing, and time did not exist. The present moment was the only thing that existed. It was the only thing that had ever existed, that ever would exist. And she existed purely in the present. Timeless. Formless.

• • •

The ring of the doorbell and the snick of the sliding deadbolt brought Vivien and the detective out of their meditative state. But not Clift. He continued to exist beyond time and the dream of form.

As Liz passed through the foyer, a gentle breeze carried in her scent. Even Vivien could smell it. Lightly floral with a background note of musk. Handmade by Buddhist monks.

VIVIEN, AFTER

Clift's body spasmed and contracted as his physical form reawakened, corrupted by Vivien. The service revolver was already in his good hand—the hand he used to nudge the joystick chair control. It had been in his hand, under the lap blanket since Vivien had placed it there thirty minutes ago. He managed to get both hands around the grip.

The detective had time to see what was happening, but there was no time to react. Perhaps he was still in a timeless state.

The first bullet entered just under Liz's jaw, on an upward trajectory, and traveled into her skull—the medulla oblongata, the lower half of the brainstem, the oldest part of the brain.

The rest of the shots went wild. The percussions were deafening, but Clift never heard them.

The physical form that was Liz's body and housed the miracle of her biological life, dropped inelegantly to the floor.

Vivien had time to consider the fact that Liz was the second person to die in that foyer.

And then she thought: *On the first shot.*

Synchronicity.

No Mask to Wear

SHE HAD TO RESPECT THE DETECTIVE. HE PRACTICED WHAT HE preached. Although, he never preached, per se.

He accepted the present moment as it was.

His department-issued service revolver was the murder weapon. He quietly and calmly told the investigators that the only person (besides himself) who had access to the gun was his wife, Vivien. He did not say that Vivien had placed the gun in Clift's hands. He made no accusations. He did not try to defend himself beyond stating the facts.

The circumstantial evidence pointed to Vivien. She had been present at both shootings. She engaged a lawyer. But what motive had she, the lawyer asked the investigators. Yes, but what motive had the detective, they replied. No motive was needed, the lawyer said. This was not murder for gain. This was not murder in any sense. It was criminal negligence. Perhaps, at worse, involuntary manslaughter.

The only fingerprints on the gun belonged to the nephew and the detective, the lawyer said. There was just no getting around that.

What there was no getting around, the investigators said, was that there was in fact a motive. As the legal guardian of her nephew, Vivien Williams stood to control a sizeable trust fund. With her first husband dead, and her second husband facing imprisonment, she stood to be rich and untethered.

Where is your proof? Make a charge with proof to back it up or stop badgering my client.

The detective went to jail. For how long or for what broken statute, Vivien did not know. She had stopped following the case.

She had Clift, the reincarnation of K, institutionalized.

J. Krishnamurti could be J. Krishnamurti equally in an institution or a suburban home.

The present moment was a moveable feast.

VIVIEN, AFTER

With no financial constraints, no societal obligations, no role to play, and no mask to wear, Vivien purchased airfare to India.

A Rather Unpleasant Jewel

SHE ATTEMPTED TO RELIVE THE PILGRIMAGE OF SPIRITUAL enlightenment that she and the detective had experienced on their honeymoon. Not *relive*—that smacked of longing for the past rather than relishing the present moment—but rather a *continuation*. She traveled the enlightenment circuit, slumming from tent to cave to ashram, meeting with one bearded, turbaned, olive-skinned guru after another. Some quite famous. Others (the cave dwellers) were less well known, but highly regarded locally and whispered about in the spiritual community.

But something was missing, and Vivien (neither her conscious-self nor her unconscious-self; neither the observer nor the observed) couldn't quite put her finger on the root of the ennui.

Perhaps she was homesick. Even though she was in the land of gurus and spiritual advisors, she found herself seeking news of America. She felt out of time and space. Normally a good thing, but she also felt out of alignment. So, she returned to her home, the site of two murders. But still the spiritual restlessness persisted. Perhaps, she thought, I'd be happier at Liz's home (which was now hers—she'd long since evicted Bruce).

But would she be happy in that house? Itself the site of murder and sexual assault.

And then her witnessing-self latched onto that word bandied about by her unconscious-self—*happy*. What was happiness and why did her ego-identified mind seek it?

Happiness.

What had that to do with contentment? She consulted her modest library of philosophical and spiritual texts. There was a great deal of talk about suffering, not so much about happiness. Surely, she had suffered. Who could claim otherwise? Suffering, the consensus seemed to be, was the true path to inner peace. The goal was not happiness, but rather peace.

VIVIEN, AFTER

She knew she was at peace, and yet the off feeling persisted. What was blocking her? What was this smudge on her serenity?

During a long session of meditation in which she had successfully silenced the chattering mind and was in a state of acceptance with the Now, the answer came to her, unbidden. It was simply there. A single-word message from beyond her reptile mind.

Guilt.

What she had been feeling was guilt.

The lizard brain did not experience guilt. Of course not. Just as God did not experience guilt. But the reptilian complex understood what was keeping Vivien from being in alignment with the universe itself.

Guilt.

It blocked access to the reptile self. The one true self.

She came to realize that her goal to be the observer of her own thoughts, to watch, witness, and observe—without judgement, without condemnation or approbation—to merely observe and thereby sense her true self behind her ceaselessly chattering, ego-derived, mind-identifying self, had been a success.

The problem (if *problem* was the correct word) was that she had denied her mind nothing. *Nothing.* No thought or ideation was forbidden. And ultimately, allowed to indulge in such thinking without judgement—without guilt—her true self had allowed her physical self to act on those thoughts and desires.

The problem now (and *problem* was most certainly the correct word), was that regret from her egoic mind was bleeding into the consciousness of her true self. Blocking her communion with the reptilian complex.

A witness is neither guilty nor innocent. It is simply a witness. Yet her witnessing-self felt guilt for what the unconscious-self had done.

The unconscious-self had done some truly wicked things.

In this current state (this fall from Grace), she could not be one with the universe. Synchronicity was impossible.

If a tsunami came along, she would not find herself on high ground, she would find herself among the soggy dead.

Where could she turn but to Krishnamurti?

K, such a harmonious spirit, a true genius, referred to guilt as "a rather unpleasant jewel." His talk on guilt was meandering (he tended to be tangential), but in the end—through the beauty of a mixed metaphor—he said that guilt was something to be accepted. It was in the turning away, the denying of it, that conflict and disharmony arose.

Greed, anger, violence, envy—are part of us. Hardwired into the brain. K didn't specifically mention the reptile brain, but Vivien knew what he meant. These things are present in the brain, yet we have been conditioned to deny them. These attributes are us. You feel greed, you feel envy, you feel the urge to kill. Yet we say no, those things are different from me. I feel anger, but I am not anger, therefore I must control it. Or I must indulge it. And in trying to control it, or indulge in it, conflict arises.

As long as you identify as *other* (other than violence, other than greed, etc.) a division exists. You are not one. It's back to the curse of duality.

So you must stay with this thing, this quality that *is* you. This greed or hatred or violence or whatever the quality might be. Stay with it. Do not resist it. K compared it to holding a magnificent, intricate jewel. Stay with it, he said. Examine every facet.

Guilt, Krishnamurti said, is not a problem, but simply a fact. You did or thought something that causes you to feel guilt. This is a fact. Hold this fact in your mind like a jewel. Stay with it. Examine it. Like a jewel. "A rather unpleasant jewel." And here he mixed his metaphors. That jewel, that rather unpleasant jewel, if you stay with it and don't resist it, but accept it—it begins to bloom, and then, as all blooms must, it withers.

Was this the secret? It made her think of William Blake and his poison tree. Had she planted a guilt tree and watered it in fears, night & morning with her tears. And sunned it with smiles, and with soft deceitful wiles.

Could her guilt tree wither and die, if she accepted the poisonous jewel-like fruit as her own?

The Eckhart Tolle Murder Club

THE DETECTIVE, SHE REALIZED, HAD ACTED AS SPIRITUAL GURU to her. She desired his guidance in this matter of guilt, and this needing of the man she had betrayed added to her guilt.

She did some research. To see if the detective remained incarcerated. Did he continue to play the role of prisoner, or was he giving an encore as a detective?

He was out and about. And quite active. She found that he had grown quite vocal post-incarceration. Giving interviews and participating in mud-raking media.

The pieces that captured her attention were the most sensationalistic.

Krishnamurti Thrill Kill Kult.

Jonathon Livingston Psycho.

The one that really caught her eye was *The Eckhart Tolle Murder Club.* It was a bit more tongue-in-cheek.

The first rule of the Eckhart Tolle Murder Club is that the present moment is all we have.

The second rule of the Eckhart Tolle Murder Club is that thought is illusory.

The future does not exist.

The past does not exist.

The present moment is all there is and all there ever will be.

All this according to once-imprisoned Detective…

It went on, but Vivien merely skimmed. The detective was now publicly denying culpability and laying the blame at Vivien's feet. Let him. She was, after all, guilty.

She was surprised he hadn't tracked her to India. Perhaps he couldn't afford the expense. His defense fees had likely drained dry any discretionary funds.

She knew where he lived. So she knocked at his door. Thirty-four minutes after midnight, she knocked at his door.

To discuss a rather unpleasant jewel.

The Blood of Jesus

"I KNOW HOW YOU DID IT," HE SAID.

As always, he was quite calm, reserved, fully conscious and completely in the present moment.

"Then there's no need to discuss it."

"You trained your nephew. Like one of Pavlov's dogs, you trained him to kill in exchange—"

"Skinner, not Pavlov. Operant conditioning. That is the past. Out of our control."

"Yes."

"In the present, in this moment, I feel—"

"What I am saying is that you used his body, you used the natural and normal urge for union in an unnatural... Do you see what I am saying. You understand, unnatural?"

"Yes, I understand."

"It is against God."

"God?"

"Yes, God. But besides God, beyond that, you took the teachings of wise men and twisted their meaning. Do you understand what I am saying to you? It is a distortion."

"Took? Took the teachings?"

"Yes, took."

"Took. Past tense. The Buddha said, 'Do not dwell in the past, do not dream of the future, concentrate the mind on the present moment.'"

"No. There you go again. This present moment is a result of the past."

"Is it?"

"Yes, it most certainly is. What you are doing is sophistry. You know that word? It means false logic."

"Logic itself is already the source of all sin, so false logic must be even worse."

"Of course it is worse. What is wrong with you? Your head. Your mind. Like a child. A petulant child."

VIVIEN, AFTER

"Children don't understand the full consequences of their actions. We are all children in the eyes of God."

"Well then you tell Him that when he casts you into the lake of fire. There is where you deserve to go. Wicked, wicked woman. Tell him you are but a child."

She looked at him for a few moments. The detective was no longer fully present. No longer in the Now. He was unconscious. Consumed with mind-identified thoughts and emotions. Anger. Violent urges. His fists were clenched. She had never seen him exhibit raw emotion. Or reference the vengeance of the Christian God.

"I'm sorry," she said. "I'm sorry you went to prison. I'm sorry I killed my husband. I'm sorry I killed my sister. I'm sorry I killed…"

"Who? That woman? You killed that woman, too. Three deaths. A trinity of death."

Vivien thought of the blinding flash of a stainless steel basin holding a bit of discarded medical waste. A fourth death. But that never happened. "That's me. Destroyer of worlds"

The detective shook his head at this mockery of the words of the multi-armed god Vishnu.

"I'm sorry I killed that welfare woman. Whoever she was."

"And what you did to Clift. You molested him. You made him a murderer. You murdered through him. You see?"

"That's the first rule of the Krishnamurti Kill Kult. Murder through other, not through self."

"You are making a joke?"

"I don't know what to do. I feel guilt."

"Guilt? You feel guilt. She feels guilt. This petulant child feels guilt."

Now he sounded like a Jewish grandmother.

"Clift is highly evolved. His path to enlightenment cannot be interrupted by you. It is through suffering that he advances, that he reaches nirvana."

"Then I have helped him."

"He was past suffering. Past desire. Your words are sophistry. Distortion. Do not use the teachings of the east to justify your wickedness."

"I have helped him. You know this to be true. All that happens is meant to happen. This, you also know to be true. My actions have propelled Clift to freedom from suffering and rebirth. He is almost there. Once as Krishnamurti, then as Clift, and now, perhaps, he is at the end. The ending of desire, and therefore the end of suffering. Nirvana."

"No. No, no, no. No. You have lit the fire of desire. you have fanned the flames and diverted this holy man from his path."

"Again, I have helped him. All that happens is meant to happen. This was meant to happen to Clift. I was meant to happen."

"You make me to have violent thoughts."

As he said those words, the detective glanced down at his wrist. As though he were glancing at a wristwatch. He wore a Theosophical Society ring on his middle finger, but there was no watch on his wrist. There was a tattoo. Vivien hadn't noticed it before, but there it was. A crude jailhouse tattoo of a cross.

A cross.

"So, you're a Christian now?" Her tone was flat but not completely neutral. It was the same tone one might employ with a declarative question such as *So, you're a nudist now?* Or *So, you're vegan now?*

He nodded.

Had the detective been saved? Had he accepted Jesus Christ (perhaps in the aftermath of a brutal assault) as his personal Lord and Savior? Had he spent late nights reading the New Testament, seeking a future salvation? A deliverance? But the detective of all people knew that salvation existed only in the present moment.

"If there is any regard left for me in your heart, I need your help so that I might move past this guilt."

"You said you *helped* Clift. That you felt no remorse."

"I don't. Not for Clift. But for William. For Liz. For that blackmailing woman. And for you. For sending you to prison."

The detective was silent for quite a long time. Then he sighed. "You are already forgiven."

"I am?"

"Yes." Again, silence. Then, "Your sins are washed away."

"I don't understand. Are you saying—"

"You are cleansed of sin."

"Through the blood of Jesus?"

"Yes. Through the blood of Jesus."

A Moon for the Misbegotten

THE DETECTIVE WAS LOST. OF NO USE TO HER. PRISON HAD ruined him. Broken him. He was the disciple of another now.

She was home, meditating (thinking no-thoughts) when the doorbell rang. She opened the door without checking. She fully accepted all circumstances life might direct to her.

She opened the door to *her* first disciple.

He was a teenage boy. The condition of his clothing, the greasy hair, and the rank body odor told her he was homeless. The odd glint in his eyes told her he was mentally ill. Unstable. A crude cardboard sign was propped behind him in the breezeway. The sign was soiled and grease-stained. Vivien couldn't make it all out. It was dense with childish block printing. Something about *the poor* and *food* and *help*.

She stood aside to let the boy enter. Thankfully he left the beggar's sign outside. But he carried in a filthy canvas knapsack, stuffed with what Vivien presumed were all the boy's worldly belongings.

Even though it was a warm day, he wore a corduroy overcoat that was far too big for him and as soiled and odorous as the boy wearing it. He reached into a voluminous pocket and held up a phone. Even the poorest of the poor had electronic devices now. The government gave them away. Probably to track the homeless—lest they find their way into the hands of those who would recruit them as insurrectionists.

On the screen was an article about Vivien. The Murders. The Krishnamurti Kill Kult. The photo of her was from an old church bulletin. Barely recognizable.

"Are you hungry?"

The young man nodded. Then he said, "They told me to come."

This gave Vivien a pause. "Who? Who told you to come."

The boy reddened and grew silent.

"It's okay. You can tell me. Who told you to come here? To me."

VIVIEN, AFTER

After what appeared to be a great deal of inner turmoil, the young man said, "Them. They told me."

There was dried spittle in the corner of his mouth.

"Who is them? Do they have a name?"

The boy shook his head, unkempt hanks of oily hair swaying.

"Okay. That's fine."

"They told me. I heard them."

"Voices? Voices told you?"

He nodded.

"Do you hear them now?"

He nodded again and said, "They're happy now. Now I'm here. With you."

"Do you take medicine?"

He nodded.

"Have you been taking it?"

He shook his head.

"Do you have it with you? Do you have your meds with you?"

He nodded and glanced at the bedraggled backpack. He opened the pack and pulled out an old cigar box. El Roi-Tan. Fresh Golfers. *The Cigar That Breathes*, it said on the side of the worn, peeling box.

"Okay. Good. But let's get you something to eat first. And maybe a hot shower after."

•••

A week later, two middle-aged women showed up. Seeking shelter. Seeking inner peace and enlightenment. Refugees from a battered women's shelter. They found Vivien's supposed act of mariticide to be inspirational. They would not give their names. They were in hiding from abusive spouses. The first said, "Just call me Charlotte." The other said, "Call me Charlotte, too." Thus, they were known as Charlotte One and Charlotte Too.

Then a man who barely spoke English.

She gave them all food and shelter. And allowed them to experience her stillness, as the detective had sought out Clift to commune in his enlightenment.

But the detective was a disciple of Jesus now. A follower of another.

Now, it seemed, Vivien had disciples of her own.

She was a guru.

Flashpoint

SHE REALIZED THAT SHE WAS LESS A GURU AND MORE OF A CULT leader (but *not* a Krishnamurti Kult).

She was a flashpoint. A beacon for the lost and misbegotten. Including those who found murder to be a spiritual act.

The soiled (and clearly schizophrenic) young man was her first disciple, and her favorite. His name was Binion Graves, but she called him Pigpen, as a joke, after the perpetually dirty *Peanuts* comic strip character.

Pigpen was her Andrew the Apostle—the first disciple to be called by Jesus. Andrew's brother, Peter, got more press coverage, but it was Andrew who first met Jesus.

Pigpen. She regretted calling him that, because the others picked up on it and started calling him that too. He didn't seem to care. Pigpen stayed in the backyard all day, digging in the dirt, finding creepy crawlies, and dropping them in that beat-up El Roi-Tan (*The Cigar That Breathes*) box.

Everybody had a nickname. Pigpen, Charlotte One and Charlotte Too, Timmie Tim, and the newest member, Sedentary Sue (who watched TV all day and seldom moved from the couch).

They called Vivien *Maddox*. Nobody said why.

She realized she was creating her own Manson Family. All they were missing was a Squeaky Fromme.

She had read that Manson purged the cult members of their old identities using drugs and extreme forms of sex to make them "empty vessels that would accept anything he poured."

Each of them was under Vivien's control to one degree or another. They were her vessels.

She could send these people out like assassins in the night if that was her desire. Ripples of evil.

But it was not her desire. Her burden of guilt was already more than she could bear.

VIVIEN, AFTER

She wanted to do good. Even though there was no such thing as good or bad. There were only life circumstances.

She did not want the responsibility. She did not want to be a guru.

She discovered Charlotte One and Charlotte Too in the backyard smoking a yellowed glass pipe of what she assumed was crack cocaine. Charlotte Too had a Russian accent and called the drug *rock*.

We are Smucking Ruck.

Both women had bad skin and missing teeth, and Vivien had assumed it was a result of either poverty or physical violence.

She smoked the rock cocaine with them.

It was heavenly.

Even now, she thought, *you are in the midst of heaven. Turn over a rock, and there you'll find me.*

She'd found heaven under a rock.

"Get more," she told the Charlottes and shoved a wad of cash into their hands. "I've got plenty of money."

It Makes You Feel Good

SHE FOUND THE CHARLOTTES IN THE UPSTAIRS BATHROOM—using it like a science lab. There was a Bunsen burner and glass beakers bubbling with a thick, noxious yellow substance. Vivien saw a pile of red match heads and blister packs of cold-medicine tablets. A bottle of Drain-O. And a bag of insulin needles.

This was too much. Even for an enlightened person who had advanced beyond self, beyond form, this was a threshold that dare not be crossed.

"It's called Krokodil. I learned make in Russia."

"It's not dangerous," Charlotte One added. "Not like you hear."

"Hear what? I've never heard of it. Crocodile?"

"They call it Krokodil because it makes your skin look like an alligator. Like green alligator skin. Scales."

Reptilian brain, reptilian skin.

"But that only happens because people cook it up with impurities. They use harsh chemicals. Charlotte Too knows what she's doing."

"It pure. The best stuff. Safe."

"How could it not be safe, with Drain-O in it?"

"No. No, no. That boil off. It burn out the impurities then evaporate. Baking soda to cut the acid. Clean. This is clean."

"What does it do?"

"It makes you feel good."

The Charlotte's injected each other at the top the pelvic area, just below the waist.

She looked at the two women and thought, *the means of death are so sweet.*

Vivien unbuttoned her pants and exposed the area.

The needle tore the skin.

Three Two One

THE FRONT AND BACK DOORS BURST OPEN AT 3:21 IN THE morning. A swarm of officers wearing heavy tactical gear entered the home.

Hearing it from her bedroom upstairs, Vivien understood what was happening.

Sitting up in bed, listening to furniture shatter and the screams of her disciples, Vivien knew the detective was in the house. She had been keeping tabs on him and knew he was back on the force. His lawyer had bargained the criminal negligence charge to below the felony level. The detective had petitioned for and received an absolute pardon, which left him eligible to apply for law enforcement, but he had to start over as a police officer. He was no longer, technically, a detective.

Although she had developed a skin ulcer just below her left hip bone, she hadn't used the Krokodil long enough to become dependent on it or, regrettably, to develop reptilian skin. Everybody in the house—except Pigpen who was permanently blissed—used the drug. The two Charlottes sold it on the street to neighborhood kids.

It was a bad scene. A bad life circumstance. Or, rather, a life circumstance that was neither good nor bad, but simply existed as it was, as the universe intended it to exist. How could it be any other way?

The press would certainly spin it as bad.

Krishnamurti Krokodil Kompound KO'd.

From McMansion to Meth Lab—What Went Wrong?

Her bedroom door opened. It didn't explode open. There were two quick raps, and then the detective walked in. He closed the door and mumbled something into his shoulder mic. He was wearing full protective gear. He motioned for her to get up.

Vivien got out of bed and stood before the detective.

With no warning, he punched her squarely on the nose. Blood poured. She was grateful for it, because in that moment, all thought ceased, and there was a pause in her internal stream of thought. And during that pause, she was fully conscious. Aware that she did not end at her skin. That she was eternal, existing beyond thought and time.

Just as she was getting back to her dream form that she mistakenly called reality, the detective struck her again. A backhand blow that spun her around.

She was again detached from body identification. And when she returned to the realm of limitation; she saw the detective remove what looked like duct tape from his duty belt. He wrapped the tape all the way around her head, over her mouth, muting her. Then he pulled a bag of some kind over her head. It went down past her shoulders. It might have been a pillowcase, but it blocked all light and extinguished sound. She felt the alarming sting of zip cuffs being pulled too tight around her wrists, binding her.

She was escorted out of the house (dragged, really) and into the dark, predawn morning. She could feel the cool air on her arms and ankles.

The detective pushed her head down and ushered her roughly into the back of a vehicle. She felt the throb of the engine as they sped away.

No Guru

SHE WONDERED IF THE DETECTIVE WAS PUNISHING HER. With the duct tape and dense head covering, he'd deprived her of sensory input. He'd made her deaf, dumb, and blind.

After a long time, the detective stopped the police cruiser. He got out and pulled Vivien from the back of the vehicle. He was gentler now. He controlled her movements, but there was a tenderness in that control.

She felt the blade against her skin before it jerked up and freed her of the zip cuffs. He removed the covering from her head. Then he used the blade again to carefully slit the tape under her jaw and peel it back from her skin. She saw the tape was slick with blood from her battered nose. Her cheek felt like it was torn open. The detective wore a silver ring with a raised relief of the Theosophical Society logo. The insignia was a mixture of ancient symbols (including a swastika) bearing the legend: THERE IS NO RELIGION HIGHER THAN TRUTH.

The truth had left a laceration on her face that felt like it would require stitches to close. She was surprised he still wore the ring after his conversion to Christ.

Even now, in her physical pain, and in the midst of a reality that was decidedly unpleasant, her mind sought out the past. The mind always, always, seeks to live in the future or the past—two places which do not exist. She remembered when she had first noticed the ring and asked him about it. He explained a little about Theosophy, but the main point was that at age fourteen, Jiddu Krishnamurti was taken in by the Theosophists and groomed as the coming Lord Maitreya—the new World Teacher, a highly evolved spiritual being meant to oversee the evolution of humanity. As an adult, Krishnamurti rejected the title and extricated himself from the Theosophical movement. He never desired to be a leader—spiritual or otherwise—and advised others to follow only themselves, to recognize only themselves as spiritual authority.

No priest, no guru, no follower.

VIVIEN, AFTER

She stood on the dark isolated street, in the damp night air, looking into the detective's eyes. He leaned forward and whispered in her ear. Then he stood back and pointed. She could see the cross tattoo on his wrist. She looked in the direction the cross pointed. After that, he got back in the cruiser and drove away, leaving her alone.

She was cold and bleeding. In need of medical attention. She had no money, no phone, no identification.

Barefoot and wearing only a nightgown, she started walking.

Sanctuary

HER DESTINATION WAS A DOMESTIC VIOLENCE SHELTER. Discretely located and passing as a typical suburban home.

She rang the bell twice and faced the security camera. She could see her reflection in the dark dome over the lens. She truly was a battered woman.

They took her in. As the detective had instructed, Vivien told them she was escaping an abusive relationship and in fear for her life. She had escaped, quite literally, with only the clothes on her back. They calmed her, cleaned her, and cared for her wounds. The nose was bloody but not broken. The cheek laceration probably could use a few stitches, but when Vivien recoiled at the idea of hospital treatment, they decided to make do with triple antibiotic cream and three Steri-Strips.

They told her she was safe. Nobody could get to her here. She was anonymous, an unknown, and she would stay that way. They had a rehabilitation program, residential transition, and for extreme cases like Vivien, they could help the victim establish a new identity. A new life, with a new name, far away from their abuser.

• • •

When he delivered her, the last thing the detective whispered to Vivien was, "John baptized with water, but you will be baptized with the Holy Spirit."

Pablum.

Odious, vomited pablum.

She knew her baptism would be by water. Water and ice.

As I Lay Dying

VIVIEN WORKED HER WAY THROUGH THE PROGRAM.
She was resistant. She wasn't like these other people. Vivien wasn't a victim. The only abuser from whom she sought escape was herself. How do you escape yourself? It was like a Zen koan. A paradox. There was no answer.

But perhaps, in seeking the answer, insight comes.

• • •

She met a group of like-minded women who gathered regularly in the basement of the group home. They were devoted to a book and acknowledged a power higher than themselves.

Vivien joined them.

∙ ∙ ∙

She received a new life, in a new place, with a new name.

∙ ∙ ∙

She let the past die. The past was not only past, but it had never existed. She forgot it. The memory decomposed like a once-living organism until it was dust. And as it lay dying, she forgot Alan Watts and Deepak Chopra. She forgot Krishnamurti and Sadhguru and *A Course in Miracles*.

She realized that she was herself. There was no deeper self, no truer self. There was just herself. It was all smoke and mirrors. Mind games. Illusions.

If there was an observer who existed beyond the form of mind thought, then who observed the observer of the mind? Who witnessed the witness? And who witnessed that witness? Who witnessed the witness that witnessed the witness? And on into infinity.

The observer *is* the observed.

VIVIEN, AFTER

It was semantics. Illusory linguistic trickery. It was, as J.D. Salinger put it, "the worst sort of sophistry."

One of humanity's most basic needs is the need to be forgiven. It starts in childhood. It's all any of us wants. To be free of guilt. Guilt corrupts. Forgiveness frees. The sophists tell us You Must Forgive Yourself. *Forgive yourself.* Move on. Forgive yourself and move past the guilt. Get on with your life. You are, at heart, a *good* person, a good person who has done mostly good in this life, but you made a mistake. A *bad* mistake. Forgive yourself for it. You absolutely must forgive yourself. Move on.

That is a complete and utter lie. Trickery. You are, at heart, a *bad* person who has done a few good things along the way. Who are you to forgive yourself? Are you a being that created itself? If so, if you created yourself, then you can forgive yourself. If not, then true forgiveness can only come from *outside* of you. Not from within. Who are you to forgive yourself? How dare you.

Imagine showing up to your murder trial, Or your rape trial. Or your murder-rape trial. And you address the court: "Your Honor, I have forgiven myself." The jurist would clear their throat, bang the gavel, and intone, "This trial is over. The defendant has forgiven themself."

Perhaps the person you injured or otherwise wronged can grant you forgiveness, and perhaps you can accept their forgiveness. Perhaps. It still doesn't erase the wrong. You make amends, and you both agree to not otherwise hold you accountable. But what if the person you wronged is not capable of granting pardon because they are dead, unborn, disabled, deafblind, or simply content to hate. It doesn't matter. Whether you're offered forgiveness or not, the wrong is still there. It can't be undone. You can't cut down a guilt tree. Even if you do, it'll grow right back. Twice as big. Each time bigger. With deeper roots. Deeper. And deeper still.

In your heart, you know you don't deserve forgiveness. The bad thing you did, you did it voluntarily. Or negligently. What bit of mind conditioning can you conduct to convince yourself you deserve forgiveness? You don't deserve it. You could scourge yourself, but when would it be enough? How much blood would need to flow before you believed the price had been paid? How deep would the scar tissue need to wind before you would earn forgiveness? No, that's not enough. The scarring would have to go deeper. Deeper and deeper still. It would never be deep enough because you can't by natural law earn forgiveness. You must be washed clean. It's a gift. It's unearned. A gift that comes at a cost. A cost we can't pay.

We exchanged the truth for a lie. A long lie—depending on one's perspective. A lie that courses through the bloodstream of the human race. Our forgiveness has already been purchased. We don't have to pay a penny. All we have to do is accept it. But we refuse.

• • •

We may be damned, we may have exchanged the truth for a lie, but at least we still have the sacred stillness of the present moment. At least we have that. This present moment. We have the now.

Yes, yes. Eckhart Tolle. *The Power of Now*. What *now*? Now does not exist. Now never will exist and it never has existed. All we truly have is the fact of the past and the promise of the future. This sentence exists only in the past. And the following sentence exists only in the future. Neither of them exist in the now. All we have is memory of the past and anticipation of the future. As time seemingly elongates, the more likely our recollections of it are to be inaccurate, and our predictions to miss the mark. In other words, we can't say with any degree of accuracy what happened one thousand years ago, or what will happen one thousand years in the future. But tighten up the timeline. Make it the length of but a single second. In the space of that one second, our memory of the beginning of the second will be equally accurate to our prediction for the end. The beginning of the second is the past, the end of the second is the future. Where does the now exist on that one-second timeline?

Where does now exist in the span of a minute? Where does it exist in the length of an hour? Is today now? This week. Perhaps this week is now.

But a second—a single second—must be now. Surely. Surely one second must be right now. *Surely*.

Do you know how many increments a single second can be divided into? An *infinite* number of increments. One second is eternal.

On the endless grid of the span of one second, where does *now* fall? Let's find that spot and we can all live in the present.

Now does not exist. *Now* is as undefinable as *human life*. We can't even agree on what constitutes a human being. When does life begin? We don't know. We really, truly do not know. Stephen Hawking, the theoretical physicist, said he regarded his brain as a computer which will stop working when its components fail. "There is no heaven or afterlife for broken-down computers; that is a fairy story for people afraid of the dark."

What if the fairy story we tell ourselves is that a human being growing inside another human being isn't a human being?

Of course, it doesn't actually matter—if there is no God. Plant life, aquatic life, animal life, human life. Just props. Organic matter bound for the compost pit. If there is no God, then we are all walking talking bags of fertilizer. Creatures waiting to be embalmed or bagged and wrapped in red biohazard tape, a discreet packet destined for a cemetery or a crematorium. Dumped into a hole in the earth or set ablaze and emitted into the sky.

Yet we need a fairy-story-god because we're afraid of the dark.

Helen Keller lived in darkness. Her childhood was a soundless, sightless void—an abyss—without communication from the world outside of herself. Upon first being told about God, Ms. Keller said, "I always knew He was there, but I didn't know His name."

If God is a shared delusion, how did Helen Keller fall prey to this mental illness?

We have been malignly misguided.

We, as a species, got off track (our separateness began) when we ate the apple from the Garden of Eden. That apple was poisoned with logic. Intellectualism. The illusion that we can forgive ourselves, define ourselves, define God. The long lie.

Vivien accepted that the poison apple was within her. But she rejected Eastern spiritualism. She rejected self-forgiveness. She rejected enlightenment. She rejected the philosophical entertainers. She rejected the past and rejected the future and rejected the present moment as well. Linguistic trickery.

She accepted her new life. Her regeneration.

The years passed and she lived the new life. The new life circumstance. She found a new life partner. With whom she enjoyed the ephemeral bliss of physical union. She told him she had gotten out of a bad marriage. Had changed her name so her abusive ex couldn't find her. (She didn't mention that her abusive ex was herself. She had already forgotten that part.) She made it clear that she preferred a private life. A quiet life. And that is what they had—a good marriage and a quiet life—until one of them died unexpectedly many years later.

She lived her new life circumstance without awareness of the old life circumstance. Free from the need to seek purpose. She had purpose. Without anticipation for what may lay ahead, or regret for what lay behind. Simply living life for the sake of living life.

The eagle soars because the eagle soars.

"The special disease of civilized man might be described as a block or schism between his brain (specifically, the cortex) and the rest of his body."

—Alan Watts
The Wisdom of Insecurity

"Let us say that on the game board—our universe in space-time—the Dark Counterplayer makes a move; he sets up a reality situation. Being the Dark Player, the outcome of his desires constitutes what we experience as evil: nongrowth, the power of the lie, death and the decay of forms, the prison of immutable cause and effect."

—Philip K. Dick
speech in Metz, France, 1977

"We might reflexively reach for a light switch in the bathroom only to discover that it was—always had been—in another place entirely ... a reflex left over from a previous present, still active at a subcortical level ... This might account for the sensation people get of having lived past lives. They may well have, but not in the past."

—Philip K. Dick
speech in Metz, France, 1977

"Before Abraham was, I am."

—Jesus Christ, Righteous Branch
John 8:58

How to Be Born Again:

{1}
Don't Want Nobody to Moan

HERE IS WHAT WE KNOW.

We know that at some point between midnight and three in the morning, the woman who existed in the physical form called Maddox Evans got out of bed and left her sleeping husband behind. We do not know what woke her, or what prompted her to get out of bed. We do not even know for certain that she had truly been asleep that night. It is possible she only pretended to sleep.

We know that she (or an unknown someone with her—highly unlikely) opened the garage and drove away. She did not close the garage door. She was still wearing her nightgown, but no slippers.

Maddie's husband, Chaplain Evan Evans, awoke at three in the morning to find his wife was not in bed, not anywhere in the house, her car gone, the garage door open. Her phone was charging on the kitchen counter. Chaplain Evans dressed and took his vehicle to go look for his wife in the frigid night. He searched for three hours. He was sick with worry, yet selfishly, he considered the fact that with the garage door open for who-knew-how-long, he would certainly be dealing with frozen pipes come daylight. He despised himself for such a self-centered thought. At a time like this. The human mind is a funny thing

When he got home, dawn was breaking, and the police were waiting for him.

Reports of a jumper had been phoned in, and Maddox's car was found abandoned in the eastbound lanes of the Walt Whitman Bridge, the driver's door wide open, the engine still running, exhaust swirling.

Swirling in the gelid air like brush strokes in a post-impressionistic painting.

It appeared she had jumped from the bridge's south side. Search efforts were called off when her body washed up on the bank of the Delaware River later that morning.

That is what we know. What we do not know is *why*.

Why would a woman not being treated for depression or any other mental illness, a woman who was not despondent in any way, a woman who gave no indication whatsoever of suicidal ideations—why would she feel such a sudden and undeniable compulsion to end her own life? A compulsion so urgent that she fled her home deep in the night, wearing only a nightgown. Why would she abandon her car in the middle of a bridge, engine idling, door open, and then unceremoniously plunge to her death?

What compelled her?

This question would plague Chaplain Evans for many years. He knew Maddie had been married before him. It had been an abusive relationship. But it certainly didn't haunt her. It was another lifetime. Forgotten. Not even a memory.

He led a community of men and women in prayer and pastoral counsel. Most were in distress. Forgotten. Misbegotten. How could he have not seen the disattunement swirling in his own wife's eyes? He only wanted to make sense of Maddie's death. He did not want to believe that he had lived with a stranger.

He felt betrayed.

{2}
True Religion in My Heart

MADDOX EVANS HAD SEEN THE HOMELESS MAN PANhandling at the top of the highway exit ramp many times before. She'd even rolled down her car window (just a crack) and given him a twenty-dollar bill close to Christmas last year. He always held a makeshift sign—a soiled square of cardboard. It usually said NEED JOB WIFE KIDS. Sometimes the sign said something different, like COMBAT VETERAN or SICK CHILD. But today the sign said something *entirely* different.

Today the sign said, YOU ARE NOT HERE.

Not only was today's message different, but it was also graffitied on using red spray paint. Red, to draw attention to the truth of the words.

You are not here.

Sitting on the exit ramp, waiting for the light to turn green so she could continue on her way home, Maddie was trapped. She couldn't look away from the sign or the homeless person holding it. When she shifted her gaze from the sign to the man, he was staring directly at her. Communication rippled between them.

He smiled. It was a knowing gaze. Like he was smiling directly at her because he had made that sign just for Maddox. A message for her alone.

Unbidden, she thought, *a hole in the earth and a vessel in the sky*.

Time seemed to stop. She prayed and prayed and prayed to Jesus for the light to turn. And finally, He answered her prayers. The light changed from red to green, freeing her. She drove home.

The whole thing disquieted her, and she kept thinking about it all evening. It preoccupied her, but she did her best to act normal around Evan. She listened to his complaints from his day at the Department of Corrections, then made dinner, and watched TV with her husband, mostly in silence, which was normal for them.

VIVIEN, AFTER

Maddie got in bed at ten. And even though it was far too cold, she got up and opened the bedroom window. Less than an inch. Just a crack. Just enough to let in sound from outside. Their backyard had a small brook (surely frozen) with a weeping willow tree growing beside it, and sometimes, at night, there was a songbird who sings. She chastised herself for thinking *small brook*. Brook already meant small. The word *brook* meant small stream. So saying (or thinking) *small brook* was superfluous. Redundant. An unnecessary use of more than one word or phrase meaning the same thing.

What a silly thought to have. She was being silly. How silly of her.

Silly or not, *brook* has more than one meaning. *Creek* or *branch* would have been a better choice. More concise. Greater clarity. We all seek clarity. But *creek* and *branch* also have more than one meaning. If she'd said (or thought) *creek*, she could have meant a native American—a Muscogee Creek. If she'd thought *small creek*, instead of *small brook*, her thought could have been misinterpreted as meaning there was a small Indian in her backyard with a weeping willow tree growing next to them. And maybe a cowboy. Cowperson. Whatever.

Her thought could have been misinterpreted, that is, if someone or something was monitoring her thoughts.

How silly and funny. *Cowperson*.

Evan came in and took a shower in the master bath. From her perch, she watched her husband emerge, glistening, from the steamy bathroom. He unwrapped the damp towel from around his middle and put on his pajamas.

Evan still had a good body. She admired that about him.

He said frazil ice was building up on the Delaware, causing a lot of excitement and a lot of headaches. He said it was a mess. Evan was worried about losing utility service. The river ice was clogging the intake system at the water plant. Even if the water stayed on, they could be dealing with burst pipes in the morning. He was worried.

She said, "You're telling the devil where your goat is tied."

Evan nodded, knowing she was right, and went back downstairs to finish watching the local news—and to set the faucets dripping.

Maddie got up and shut the bedroom window. The songbird was nowhere to be found. Perhaps it didn't like the cold. She hadn't seen that songbird in quite a while. Years. Nor had she heard it. Or felt joy from its sweet, simple trill. Perhaps it had flown south for the winter. And what kind of bird sings only at night?

She, herself, preferred the light. Maddie was drawn to the light.

Last spring, she had been mowing the lawn, and stopped the mower near the murky, foul-smelling brook. She saw three miniature eggs under the weeping willow—cracked, broken. Discarded. They looked like tiny, crushed skulls. She knew birds would sometimes destroy their own eggs. The behavior was known as egg tossing. The bird perceived the eggs as defective or otherwise undesirable. Unwanted. So they destroyed them. Destroyed their own eggs. But what kind of animal did such a thing?

In bed, pulling the covers up to her chin and turning off the light, she remembered the rancid odor of the stagnant brook.

Maddie tried to clear her mind. She needed to sleep. No more thoughts of foul-smelling water, goat-stealing devils, or battered bird eggs.

Still, she wished it would come back. Someday, maybe. She missed that songbird.

The human mind is a funny thing. It tricks us. It tells us lies sometimes.

Later, Evan climbed into his side of the bed. He said, "It's spitting snow. Flurries."

She didn't respond. Pretended to sleep. Evan kissed the back of her neck and whispered, "'Night, Emmie." It was his pet name for her. M.E. *Emmie*. He turned onto his side, facing away from her. Soon, Evan's deep, even breathing matched her mock susurrations of sleep.

Her mind was racing.

Lying in bed, ME considered reaching for the half of an Ambien tablet that was sitting on her bedside table and letting it melt under her tongue. It might stop the humming before it started. She decided against it and then decided that the fact that the homeless man was looking directly at her was just a coincidence—a simple matter of chance. He likely made eye contact with various drivers to guilt them into giving.

Guilt.

Guilt was a powerful motivator.

She used to feel guilty for her inability to conceive a child. They had even sought medical intervention—in vitro—to no avail. In the end, Evan comforted her by saying, "'Blessed are the barren, and the wombs that never bore, and the breasts that never gave suck.'" As clergy to inmates, her husband knew the scriptures cold. She could have done without the breast-sucking imagery, but it was from the Bible. In red. Still, she felt guilty.

The reproductive endocrinologist told Maddie that in her case, in vitro fertilization was a long shot. The fertility specialist had noted "significant scarring" in Maddie's uterus. Upon the pronouncement, there was a pause—as though the doctor thought Maddie might fill in the missing blank. But Maddie said nothing. She had no memory of any incident, illness, or mishap that might have caused uterine scarring, but at the same time there *was* a quasi-déjà vu sensation (like a transparency overlay) of her adolescent breasts, tender, swelling. But no, they certainly never gave suck.

Childless. Barren. Desolate.

It all amounted to the same thing. Like creek, branch, and brook.

The fruit was blighted.

The doctor sighed and said, "Asherman's syndrome. Intrauterine adhesions. Often caused by a D&C or D&E. If somebody did this to you, they should be sued."

Maddie said nothing. She had no idea what the doctor was referring to.

"Asherman's can be treated. Hysteroscopy. Balloon catheter for two weeks. A short course of estrogen. I've seen many positive outcomes. If we get all of the adhesions, there's a very good chance you'll be able to get pregnant. On your own. And carry full term."

Maddie declined the treatment and never told Evan. It was her body, after all. Her body, her choice.

She felt guilty for not telling him.

Guilt. A word that hummed. Even now, just thinking of the word, Maddie felt a deeper sense of shame wash over her. Intense shame for some unremembered wrong she may or may not have committed. It didn't matter, though. Maddie knew we were each conceived in sin and shaped in iniquity, and so she would always feel the dark shadow of guilt passing overhead like a bird of prey. But she also knew that through the sacrifice of another, she had been washed clean.

Probably, guilt was a key tenet of panhandling—with or without eye contact. She had just never bothered to look at the man's face before. Even when she had given him that twenty-dollars last Christmas, she hadn't looked directly at him. She had slid the bill through the window crack while pretending a preoccupation with the car instrument panel prevented her from otherwise engaging with him. Nonetheless, *he* engaged with *her*. She felt and heard the rustle of his calloused fingertips snatching the currency, and she sensed the warm, germ-laden puffs of his breath as he brought his befouled lips to the barely-open glass and said, "Thank you, ma'am. I thank you. I surely thanks you."

Maddie kept her attention focused on the display screen, as though she were entering a mission-critical GPS coordinate or perhaps transmitting code to dismantle a nuclear warhead. She never turned toward the man. Not once did she look at him. She just waved her hand in his direction as if to say, *it's nothing, no big deal, now please go about your day while I finish disarming this bomb*.

But the man continued talking through the quarter-inch gap. He said, "I'll 'member you, ma'am. I'll remember your kindness. Even when I's dead and gone, I'll 'member you."

VIVIEN, AFTER

For God's sake, couldn't the man see she was engaged with something important on her vehicle's media panel? Lives could be at stake.

Still, he kept on. "And you 'member me, too, ma'am. Don't 'dismember me. You 'member me. Remember me when you come into your kingdom. And I'll remember you when I's dead and—" A horn honked behind her. Traffic had shifted forward. Still not looking at the man, Maddie took her foot off the brake. The imaginary IED successfully defused, she drove away, not giving him so much as a courtesy glance in the rearview mirror. What was he to her? What did she owe him? The man was nothing more than a common thief and could be a murderer for all she knew, not to mention mentally ill—*remember me when you come into your kingdom*. Why did it seem like she was always the flashpoint for the damaged, the outcast?

Today just happened to be the first time Maddie had taken it upon herself to really look at him. To engage in the transference of guilt—which was the man's stock-in-trade.

So probably (in all likelihood) he hadn't made the sign specifically for her. Which was just a crazy thought to have. The kind of thought that was indicative of what the Koreans referred to as *attunement disorder*. It was the kind of thought you took medicine for.

Regardless, the sign really did say YOU ARE NOT HERE.

And thinking about that got Maddie to thinking about the nature of reality. If you're not here, then where are you? *Here*, after all, is what we know. *Here* is the one place we're always guaranteed to be.

Here is what we know.

You are not here.

Okay, fine, you are not here. Then where are you?

She saw a video recently. Posted by a bearded, disheveled, dandruff-flaked man with a legion of followers. She wasn't sure how the video ended up in front of her eyes, but it had. And she watched part of it. Just enough to know it wasn't a message intended for her—not for Maddox Evans. Not for ME. The man said that none of us are here. He said that, statistically, it was very likely that what we call reality is a quantum-generated simulation.

A game.

Our universe is a simulation. That's what he said.

That we live inside a computer created by a computer created by a computer created by a computer. A child's game played by an alien toddler. A multiverse of toddlers existing in a multiverse of multiverses. Each a simulation inside a simulation.

A hole in the earth and a vessel in the sky.

Then she got to thinking about what would happen to the machine if one of the simulated beings—her for instance—did something the creator/programmer didn't foresee. But there would almost certainly be a failsafe built into the program. An infinite number of possibilities for every person. A googolplex of fates. Just for starters.

But what if, Maddie wondered, what if the creator/programmer didn't develop an algorithm (or whatever) based on the virtual beings becoming conscious of the fact that they were virtual beings? What would happen if simulated beings became aware that they were not real?

They would cease to exist. They would have to. The system would crash.

You can't continue to exist once you realize that, in fact, you do not exist.

Here is what we know. You are not here.

But because doubt existed, and doubt would always exist, maybe there was no way for the simulated entities to truly *know* they were virtual. They would always doubt it. There would always be some degree of uncertainty. Just like with religion. Even lying here now, feeling that she was on the cusp of making the most significant of discoveries—on the cusp of glimpsing God—Maddie had doubt. The only way to erase the doubt would be to test reality with the knowledge that it wasn't real. To prove you are not here. But how do you test reality? How do you prove you are not here?

Maddie felt within herself a spiritual awakening. An epiphany. She felt that the fate of every living thing in the universe was in her hands. Because they did not live, and they did not know it. They were like sheep. Electric sheep. Maybe the human mind was just a computer. What if these thoughts she was having were a delusion, because the components of her brain were starting to fail? What if she was a broken-down computer?

But, it could also be that she was among the vanguard that was trying to escape, to break the chains of electric slavery. Maybe someone (or something) had hacked the multiverse and programmed that homeless man to rewrite his sign and hold it up for Maddie to see. But if somebody could do that, why not just reprogram Maddie directly? Maybe, she thought, maybe not every human was fully formed (given freewill) as she was. Maybe some humans were just window dressing, set decoration, stage props for the other humans who had been designed with autonomy. That would explain it. It would be a lot easier to hack into a less sophisticated program—like that unhoused person. Freewill had to be quite complex to code.

That would make those with freewill and autonomy the dark players of the game. Cunning opponents. Like Caligula, Napoleon, Stalin, Hitler, Mengele, Dahmer, Jim Jones, Jane Roe—dark players all.

VIVIEN, AFTER

But did a dark player necessarily have to be a force of perceived evil? Could a dark player not simply be a disrupter of the game? A source of enlightenment, a source of human awakening. Weren't Buddha, Mohammad, and Krishna agents of disruption? Weren't *they* dark players?

A game was only fun if it was challenging. So you had to have worthy opponents. Cunning opponents. Like Jesus Christ. Jesus was a dark player.

And Maddox Evans. She was a disruptor. ME was a dark player, too.

Prompt: Jesus is light. There is no darkness in Him. How can Jesus be a dark player? How can Jesus exist in both states—light and dark—simultaneously?

Response: A fundamental principle of quantum mechanics is that quantum objects can exist in multiple states at once, a phenomenon known as quantum superposition. This means that until a measurement is made, a particle can be considered to be in a combination of all possible states.

Prompt: Can Jesus be both light and dark? Please be precise. Nothing with physics or logic.

Response: The Christian theological answer is: No, Jesus cannot be both light and dark in moral or spiritual nature. He is wholly and perfectly

good, without sin or moral contradiction. In
regards to Jesus as a "Dark Player," if you're
asking whether Jesus could ever act with hidden
motives, moral ambiguity, or evil intent—the
answer within Christian doctrine is a firm no.
Jesus is unchanging (Hebrews 13:8), sinless, and
fully aligned with the will of the Father.

Jesus is light. There is no darkness in him. Jesus is who the Dark Player is playing against. Jesus lay down His life for the sheep and started an echo that reverberates still. Would Maddie be willing to do the same? Would she be willing to play against the Dark Player?

It was her move. She could win. But in order to win, she would have to remove doubt. In order to remove doubt, she knew, you must first remove logic.

The fate of everything rested with her.

{3}
Goin' on Down to the River

AT 12:34 A.M., MADDOX GOT OUT OF BED, WENT DOWNSTAIRS to the garage, and drove to the Walt Whitman Bridge. Her head was humming, and it wouldn't stop. She was not allowing herself to think using intellect or logic. Logically, what she intended was a bad idea. So she made her thoughts no-thoughts. She plugged into her reptilian brain. The Source Code.

Her head vibrated like a tuning fork.

And it all came back to her. Her past life. Her past *lives*. She had done all of this before. But at the same time, she hadn't. Not in a literal sense. What she was experiencing wasn't an actual memory or an actual memory lapse, but rather the sense that the past wasn't past yet, because it didn't exist. Or, rather, the past was happening *right now*, and it would happen again tomorrow. Galaxies swirled just as eagles soared and she swirled and soared with them. And the reptilian brain served this, illuminated this.

The deaf, dumb, and blind reptilian brain swirls soundlessly and in stillness soars.

The greatest, most insightful thought is no-thought. *That* is enlightenment.

You cannot have enlightenment if you are aware of being enlightened.

She realized she knew the answer to the question she had asked long ago. The purpose of life is death. We are born so that we may suffer and die. It was obvious. A child could see the truth of that.

Jesus said, "I praise you, Father, Lord of heaven and earth, because you have hidden these things from the wise and clever, and revealed them to little children." And to Maddox Evans. She was as a child. God had revealed these truths to her as well.

There is no religion higher than truth. Now is the acceptable time.

VIVIEN, AFTER

Her head hummed like an overclocked GPU given a computational task beyond its processing abilities.

Overclocking essentially increases the GPU's core and memory clock speeds, allowing it to process more data per second. This can lead to improved performance in GPU-intensive tasks like gaming, 3D rendering, and virtual reality. However, overclocking also presents potential risks, including reduced lifespan and instability. A symptom of life. Mental and environmental change.

```
# Assign values or symbolic meaning:
A = "Here is what we know"
B = "You are not here"
# Create the 'equation'
equation = f"{A} = {B}"
# Display it
print(equation)
location_spacetime = ["here"]
If_you_are == ["not here"]:
    print("Here is what we know")
else:
    print("You are not here")
message
=f"
{entity1}
{entity2}
{entity3}"
print(message)
```

```
Entity1 = "Here is what we know"
Entity2 = "You are not here"
Entity3 = "We know where you hear the star tone"
{LOSS OF [I]OTA ==
LOSS OF SELF ==
THE END OF ME}
{[T]AU GAINED ==
CROSS GAINED ==
SO SWEET THE MEANS OF DEATH}
Print(final message)("1234321")
These things are preprogrammed into us.
# Abstract logic-style variables:
H = "what we know"
U = "you"
P = False   # P:
presence of "you" =>
False means "you are not here"
# Logical implication or equivalence
# "What we know"
is that "you are not here"
# Come fold my dying arms
knowledge = H
truth = not P  # You are not here
print(f"{knowledge} = not {U} present")
```

Here is what we know. You are not here. We are what is here. Here you know not. Not here you know. What is here we are. Here is not what we are. Here you know. Are we what is here? You know here not. Is what we are not here? You know here. Here, here, is not what you know we are. Know what is here is not what you are not what we are not you

VIVIEN, AFTER

are not we are not you are not we are not you are not we are not you are not here not here not here not here not here not here not here not here not here not here

S   W   I   R   L

Please, God, let it stop. Let the humming stop.
It didn't stop. It never stopped. The humming went on forever. The humming overtook her.

• • •

Maddie exited her vehicle, climbed the guardrail, and edged onto the weathered green girder. Cars lined up to watch the barefoot woman wearing only a thin nylon nightgown in subzero weather who sure looked like she was going to jump from the WWB.

Spidery, powdery snowflakes, like fluff, like cattail seed, floated—seemingly random—in the air, drifting in and out of the headlight beams. The final few remnants of confetti falling from a balcony after the last of the revelers had gone in and succumbed to sleep.

Hugging a suspender cable, Maddie was aware of being recorded. This would be on the news. *Intake System at Local Water Plant Clogged by Human Remains.* Evan might see it. Evan Evans. A repetition of a very common name. Hardly a name at all. No, this was too graphic, too disturbing for broadcast. At the very least they would blur out her face. Maybe it would end up uncensored, on a dark site. The kind of site the federal government monitors. The kind of site that sideloads malicious code.

She peered over the drop. It was golden, blue-gold, dark, like looking into a glacial abyss. With the light behind her, she imagined she could see her reflection in the icy water far below. Her image. Silhouetted in the streetlight. Reflected in the water, but not retained by it.

The abyss gazed back as she gazed into the abyss. A great, sightless, unblinking eye.

I am laying down my life so I may take it up again. No one takes it from me, but I lay it down on my own.

She observed the observer. And inched forward to meet it.

Toes over the edge, she heard the low static slush and slurry of agitated frazil crystals. The river was pregnant with ice. Somehow—miraculously—rising through the arctic night air, an updraft, toasty and somehow smelling of vanilla and honey, caressed her. A parental embrace. With the warm, welcoming aroma of a busy bakery. Like hugging your mother's apron after she's taken the cookies out of the oven.

Feels pretty good up here.

Pretty good up here.

But the embrace grew cold, callous. The honeyed air became a putrid funeral-parlor perfume. To mask the odor of rotting flesh.

VIVIEN, AFTER

She knew cold and callous was what she deserved. Putrid death was her well-earned wage.

Because it feels pretty bad down here. In herself. Cold and callous. Frozen.

Down here, her heart was in a state of frost-bitten decay, as cold and calloused as a farmer's winter-harvest hands. Her hearing had grown dull so that her ears could not listen. She had closed her eyes and could not see. Yes, it feels pretty bad down here. Dark, silent, alone.

Down here, her days were a blank without past, present, or future, without hope or anticipation, without interest or joy.

Down here, where the cattail snow floated just out of her reach, and the abyss awaited. The unseeing, unhearing, unfeeling abyss had limitless patience. It could wait forever. Because it did not know it was waiting.

She wanted to see with her eyes and hear with her ears and understand with her heart. She wanted the songbird to return to its tree by the brook, by the creek, by the branch. She wanted to turn back. Climb down. Try again. One last time. She was *good*. There was good within her. Surely, as a human being, there must be something in her worth saving. But she knew it was too late. She deserved this. She did not deserve redemption. She did not deserve a brook or a creek or a branch. She certainly didn't deserve a songbird—its sweet, simple trill a vessel of joy. She did not deserve joy. She was misbegotten. A wretch. A wicked wretch. Too undeserving of mercy. Beyond saving. Beyond forgiveness. Beyond Grace.

This is exactly what she deserves.

• • •

Rerouting Connection: In Christian theology, Jesus Christ is understood as the "Branch of God and Man." Not a creek. Not a brook. He is the Righteous Branch embodying both divine and human natures. This concept, often referred to as the hypostatic union, means Jesus is fully God and fully human, existing as one person with two distinct natures.

502 Bad Gateway: No, "creek," "brook," and "branch" are not exactly the same, though they refer to small, natural, flowing bodies of water. Generally, they indicate size, with a brook being the smallest, followed by a branch, then a creek. However, these distinctions are not strict, and the terms are often used interchangeably or based on regional naming conventions and local history. So, in that regard, yes, one could reasonably say it all amounts to the same thing.

Scanning Registry: Brook Kidron, based on biblical accounts and archaeological findings,

VIVIEN, AFTER

is a seasonal stream that flows near the hill outside Jerusalem's walls where Jesus Christ was crucified. The Gospel of John mentions Jesus and his disciples crossing the Kidron Valley on their way to the Garden of Gethsemane, shortly before the crucifixion.

Analyzing: The Kidron Valley played a role in Temple rituals, with Brook Kidron serving not only as a drainage point for the city of Jerusalem's waste, but also as a flowing vessel of the rotting detritus and blood of animals sacrificed on the altar. This association may have been significant in the context of Jesus' sacrifice.

Malware Detected: In a 19th century sermon, Reverend Charles Spurgeon describes Brook Kidron as a "most foul and filthy ditch." Brook Kidron was the open sewer for Jerusalem's temple and a place of disgrace. Spurgeon connected the physical filth of Brook Kidron to spiritual impurity and disgrace, illustrating a path of humiliation for Jesus.

Repartitioning: Spurgeon went on to say: "When houses were purged and cleansed, the filth was thrown into the Brook Kidron. The passing, therefore, over that foul and black brook becomes the symbol of a time of deep sorrow and acute distress... The King, Himself, also passed over the Brook Kidron. The royal road lies over the place of sorrow. The way, even for kings, is by the brook of grief and shame. Let us think over that thought for a while."

Reallocating: While we think over that thought for a while, let us also consider that ZAVIT, modern-day Israel's science and environment news agency, reports that, "The raw sewage of the Old City is dumped into the Kidron Creek channel. The stream located in the valley only appears during the winter, when rainfall causes the area to flood. Otherwise, there is just a flow of sewage due to a lack of infrastructure to treat it." It would seem, Brook Kidron has always been and will always be a most foul and filthy ditch.

Threat Contained: 1 Peter 2:24 and Galatians 3:13 refer to Jesus as being "hung on a tree." The Greek word for "tree" is the same word that is used for "cross," creating a theological connection that transforms the instrument of suffering into a symbol of salvation and eternal life. Peter writes: He himself bore our sins in his body on the tree, that we might die to sin and live for righteousness; by His wounds you have been healed.

Endpoint Isolation: In light of the overwhelming theological and archeological evidence—not to mention the eye-witness testimony of John—we know that Jesus's path to the cross (the tree) passed over Kidron Creek channel (that foul and black brook). Theologians have pointed out the harmony (or synchronicity) that a tree caused the Fall of man (original sin), and so, too, the

VIVIEN, AFTER

Son of man died on a tree as the second Adam—reversing the poison of sin that infected the entire human family.

Remote Rendering: So, yes, it would be accurate to say Jesus Christ died on a tree by the brook. A tree that bore the Righteous Branch, by the brook of grief and shame.

●●●

But she didn't want what she deserved. She desired a different outcome.

As she stood and peered into the Delaware River {*Kidron's gloomy stream*} her hands were numb, her arms stiff like wood, and her feet felt fused to the frozen fabricated metal of the frame girder. She was either going to die in the fall or freeze to death.

CAPTCHA: "You are not so happy as you once were. Well, it may be you are passing over your Kidron. Ah, we do not like going over Kidron. When it comes to the pinch, how we struggle against suffering…"

Maybe she could be like the woman in the Bible. The bleeding woman. Bleeding for twelve years. Reticulations of blood down her thighs. Impure. Unclean. Too stained to touch Jesus. The reticulated woman didn't dare sully Him with her unclean touch. She did not deserve His touch. So she reached out and brushed the hem of His cloak. A quick, furtive, glancing brush. Jesus felt the power go out from Him. And the reticulated woman was delivered of her bleeding. "Your faith has healed you. Go in peace and be freed from your suffering."

The suffering doesn't have to go on forever.

I'll touch Jesus.

If Maddie could catch one of those inconsequential, beautiful, sacred snowflakes, it would be like touching Jesus. Without soiling Him with her impurity or chilling Him with her frozen state. If she could just catch one of those floating cattail seeds of snow.

If she could catch one, and it melted in her hand, that would prove she wasn't frozen. It would prove that she was warm. That she was capable of giving life.

I'll touch Jesus.

But she was afraid the snowflake wouldn't melt at her touch, because she truly was cold and devoid of life. But she had to try. She had to try and touch Jesus. Had to try, had to try, had to try. So she could die easy. This was her last chance.

There was one there. Coming out of the dark night. Floating. Spidery and white. Right there. It was so close. Salvation was so close. If she couldn't earn it, maybe she could take it. Like the bleeding woman.

VIVIEN, AFTER

The wind whisked the snowflake away. Then there was another one. Floating. Moving toward her. Carried to her by the sound of a voice. A familiar voice, the sound waves pushing the icy puff closer to her. So, so close. She had to time it just right. Closer. It floated closer. Up, down, left, right, here, there. Tantalizing her.

I'll touch Jesus.

It was right there. *Right there.* In the middle of the air.

She had to at least try.

• • •

During that final moment of biological life, her brain, her human brain—the cortex—sent out a message. An energy wave. A thought that rippled like a water strider's capillary crests, spreading unheeded, unnecessary, over her reptilian mind.

The message was that the first second would never end. (Because eternity is *now*, you understand that, surely you understand.) The first second of the first minute of the first hour of her first day in hell had given birth—to the first second of something else.

The first second births the second. Which births the second. Which births the second.

The witnessing-self heard a voice swirl, pushing the sparse snow puffs through the starry night. Speech Sounds. Coarse word-symbols, uttered in a forgotten language. Words spoken in a tongue the world never recorded. The witnessing-self did not know whether the woman herself spoke these words from the precipice, or if they were carried here from a previous present. Energy waves from another millennium.

"*Remember me,*" the voice insisted.

"*Remember me when you come into your kingdom.*"

• • •

The witnessing-self witnessed the woman jump to her death.

• • •

Maddie's descending form—a straight iron nail—pierced the membranous surface of her kingdom of water and ice. Deeper. She continued into eternity. Deeper. She continued being with the universe. Deeper. As she always had and always would. Her *isness*. A being on a journey that was not a journey. A journey that had never started and would never end.

• • •

Falling from the sky, a vessel blazed—blinding. A great schism wrenched open the earth.

VIVIEN, AFTER

Hemispheres separated. Pangea split. Glaciers surged.

The sky hardened. Mountains collapsed. Oceans disgorged upon the land.

The sun dimmed and became black as sackcloth.

The moon bloomed ink-red domes of blood.

The stars spun and the Dark Player moved.

• • •

A tomb-like stillness followed—after the flood, after the cataclysm, after the splitting of the veil. In the sacred stillness of the present moment, beneath the vast vault of sky, from deep within a wound in the earth, a bird sang out. The sweet, simple trill bringing joy to anyone with ears to hear.

Its song unanswered, the bird took wing.

It flew out of the chasm, seen by no one, observed only by the great, sightless, unblinking eye of the abyss. The bird floated, alone, in the middle of the air, held aloft by the putrid updraft.

• • •

If there was a creator who had created the bird, it did not know. Nor did it wonder. It did not know its lilting trill was sweet and simple. It did not know its song brought joy.

It did not know there was an abyss.

It did not know the abyss was filled with the fragile bones of the dead.

•••

Descending out of the calcified sky, a cross-shaped shadow passed over the songbird. The threat slipped silently overhead, not even a whisper, and then the shadow returned. The avian brain lit up with a signal of danger.

But it was too late. The predator picked the smaller bird out of the sky. Its talons were long and sharp and punctured the songbird's flesh, crushing its hollow bones, killing it midair.

Merging back into the cloudless dome, the eagle released its kill, discarding the carcass into the abyss. It would return for the carrion later. Leaving the bones to the next scavenger.

For the songbird, the dream of form ended.

Nature became cursed and the poison of sin infected the entire human family.

—Billy Graham
How to Be Born Again

My days were a blank without past, present, or future, without hope or anticipation, without interest or joy.

—Helen Keller

I stood still, my whole body's attention fixed on the motions of her fingers as the cool stream flowed over my hand. All at once there was a strange stir within me—a misty consciousness, a sense of something remembered. It was as if I had come back to life after being dead ... Is it not possible that our entrance into heaven may be like this experience of mine?

—Helen Keller

No eye has seen, no ear has heard, and no mind has imagined the things that God has prepared for those who love him.

—1 Corinthians 2:9

Women received back their dead—raised to life again.

—Hebrews 11:35

Ω

THE HUMMING STOPPED. THAT WAS THE FIRST BLESSING. Which birthed the second.

THERE WAS A STRANGE STIR WITHIN HER—A MISTY consciousness. A sense of something remembered. As if she had come back to life after being dead.

THEN: DARKNESS CAME.

Then: *The stars. My God, the stars.*

Then: Light. Expanding without movement. Immeasurable and nameless. Beloved.

The light that is over all things.

She merged with the light.

It is finished.

Cleansed of sin, the dream of form ends.

Woman, here is your son.

Afterword

My apologies to Eckhart Tolle. Vivien grossly distorts his teachings.

Several chapter titles use lyrics (italicized) from the song, "Jesus Make Up My Dying Bed." Blind Willie Johnson recorded a blues version in 1927, which inspired countless others.

My thanks to the late Philip K. Dick, the late Alan Watts, the late J. Krishnamurti, and the living God, Jesus Christ.

Then another sign appeared in heaven: There was a great fiery red dragon having seven heads and ten horns, and on his heads were seven crowns. His tail swept away a third of the stars in heaven and hurled them to the earth. And the dragon stood in front of the woman who was about to give birth, so that when she did give birth, he might devour her child.

—**Revelation 12:3-4**

www.ingramcontent.com/pod-product-compliance
Lightning Source LLC
LaVergne TN
LVHW030318070526
838199LV00069B/6492